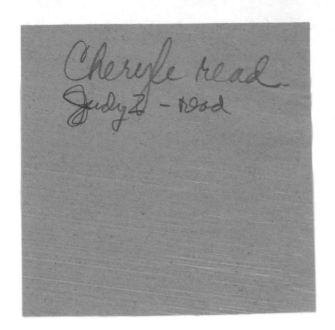

Cheryle read -
Judy Z - read

Cornered!

Nice to meet you!

Patricia Curren

Patricia Curren

ISBN: 1544982887
ISBN-13: 9781544982885

Chapter 1

Kendra Morgan's mind raced in time with the tires of the five-speed bike Mom had found at a neighborhood yard sale. She pumped her lungs full of the air that smelled like freshly laundered cotton from the afternoon's spring rain. The downpour had stopped and all that remained was the drip, drip, drip from the trees and shrubs, and the muddy puddles she splashed through. As always, she was thrilled that Johnny had called: Today he said he was finished with his chores and wanted to meet downtown to hang out.

Rounding the corner of Sycamore Street and Main, she spotted him leaning against the front of Mickey D's. Her breath caught in her throat as she stowed her bike next to his in the rack. She smoothed her blonde fly-away hair and wondered if her new T-shirt looked okay. "Hey," she said.

"Hey, yourself." He walked over and took her hand. "Wanna go for a walk?"

"Sure." She'd been with Johnny for months now and she never tired of spending time with him. Not just because of his extreme cuteness, but because he could talk about things besides cars and sports.

They meandered down the weed-filled sidewalk, barely noticing the small shops they passed. As they neared the edge of town, cracks and buckles appeared in the sidewalk and eventually it disappeared altogether. They passed a feed lot with one of the many metal buildings that dotted the countryside. She peered inside at the round hay bales stacked thirteen or fourteen high. They reminded her of giant rolls of scratchy toilet tissue. A herd of Holstein cattle bent their necks to the feed trough and slapped their tails from side to side in a useless attempt to discourage the ever-persistent flies. Johnny tugged her along to the railroad track and on to their favorite make-out spot, the old grain elevator.

Dandelions and new grass grew tall around the weathered boards of the granary. Kendra said a silent thank you for spring. She hated the cold. The past winter had been super-bad, even by Nebraska's standards.

Johnny leaned her against the rickety wall of the building and bent to brush her lips.

All thoughts of the gentle spring day dissolved. She stood on tiptoe and reached her arms around Johnny's neck to return his kiss.

He took a step back and teased, "You know, I think I could get my arms around you twice. When are you gonna start growing?" She never knew what to say to his kidding. It wasn't something she was used to. She didn't have any brothers and Dad was a big zero in the humor department, and in every other department, for that matter.

"Come on." His voice sounded hoarse. He pulled her through the big sliding door into the dim light.

She was glad this was a granary and not a hayloft, because her knees felt rubbery. *No good place to lie down.* Johnny's iPhone chirped.

"You gonna get that?"

He pulled it from his pocket and looked at the caller i.d. "Just Josh. I'll call him back." His hands moved over her shoulders and back and then down to her waist. "I like hangin' with you, Kenny."

She loved his pet name for her. "Same here." The kissing and petting continued until she felt she was falling down a deep, deep well. She could barely make out Johnny's phone ringing again. *Jam on the brakes before things get totally crazy.* "Should get back," she breathed.

Disappointment showed clearly on Johnny's face, but he nodded and brushed her fine hair back from her forehead. He yanked his phone out. "Hmm. Bryce this time." As he started to hit the call back feature, it rang again. "What the hell? Caleb now." He threw her a puzzled look. "How come you guys are blowin' up my phone?" he said into the cell. "What? You're kiddin', right?"

She stared at Johnny. *What's going on?*

"Wait a sec. I'm puttin' you on speaker. Kenny's here. Say that again."

Caleb's voice crackled over the phone. "Somethin's happened on the farm one over from you. Word is there's a woman dead. Cops are swarmin' all over the place."

"Wow! Meet us at Mickey D's."

Together, they jogged back and Kendra grabbed a booth while Johnny waited in line. As he slid a Coke over to her,

Caleb, Bryce and Josh hurried through the door and piled into the booth across from them.

Without so much as a hello, Caleb sputtered, "So, if the cops are there — means something's seriously messed up, right?"

"Not necessarily. You know the cop shop. Not much happening. Probably bored out of their minds," Johnny said. "Probably a false alarm."

But something in Johnny's tone made her fearful. She grabbed his hand under the table and fought back the frightful memories of what had happened to her last winter. Now the killer was behind bars and awaiting trial in Omaha, and Finchville's residents could sleep at night. *Except for me. And now something else bad?*

"Whadja know about them?" Caleb asked. "Didn't you tell me the cops have been there before?"

She looked at the blank expressions on Johnny's friends' faces, and then turned to him. "You saying her husband hurt her?"

Johnny shrugged. "Yeah, they've been out a coupla times. That's what my folks think."

Suddenly the buzz of excited conversation all around her filled her ears. She saw old Mrs. Michaels, eyes blazing with the thrill of something scandalous to talk about. The woman's loud whispers to the others in the next booth made her feel like the air was being sucked out of the room. She looked around her — yes, everyone was gossiping about what had happened at Johnny's neighbors. *I've got to get out of here.*

He seemed so cool about the situation. Trying to hide the terror she felt, she said, "Hey, I'm gonna take off."

"K, catch ya' later." He stood so she could slide out of the booth.

When she reached the door, he yelled, "Hey, when you gettin' a cell phone?"

"Soon as I have enough money saved." she called over her shoulder and burst through the door and out into the fresh air. She began to feel better as she pumped her bike as hard as she could, putting the disturbing scene behind her. But she still needed to talk to someone — her best friend, Audrey. She thought about how she needed someone like her — always reliable, play-it-safe, stay-out-of-trouble Audrey. As it was, her own impulsive behavior still landed them in some jams, but at least her friend managed to clamp down on some of her hare-brained ideas. The trouble was, her BFF seemed to be jealous of Johnny. Definitely out of character for her steadfast friend, but there it was.

And now that winter was gone and the grass was growing, she and Audrey could start up their lawn service again so she could get that cell phone Johnny bugged her about. As she arrived at the Worth residence, her friend appeared at the door before she could lean her bike against the porch. "Get in here, girl! You heard what happened?"

"'Course — the whole place is buzzing. That's why I'm here. I was with Johnny. He was so laid back about it. —He and his buds wanted to talk about what went down, but I was too freaked."

A smug look passed over Audrey's face. "Come on. Let's go to my room."

As usual, her friend's bed was made to perfection and not a thing was amiss in the humongous bedroom with the equally huge walk-in closet. Kendra knew if she slid open the closet door, she'd see everything arranged by type of garment and then by color. Shoes would be hung on shoe trees. Purses would be lined up neatly on the overhead shelves. She thought of her own room and how it was the polar opposite. Audrey sat cross-legged on her bed and pointed to a spot beside her. "'K, so talk. You afraid?"

She hugged herself. "Yeah, guess I am. It's bringin' up a load of bad stuff from before. And Johnny lives so close to that house!"

Audrey nudged her and said, "Your mind always goes to the dark. I'm sure he'll be fine. Come on, let's go torment my brother." She smiled and pulled Kendra off the bed, giving her a noogie as they headed to the family room.

She wondered what new bother was in store for Tyler today. It seemed like her friend morphed into a totally different person with him. Even though he was older, Audrey always knew how to work him. They found him sitting on the edge of the sofa, bent over his favorite video game, intent on destroying some weird-looking creatures.

"Hey, Tyler," Audrey said. No response. She marched over and tapped him on his shoulder. He jerked away, flailing his arm at her while he continued to fire at the screen.

"Get outta here," he grunted. "I'm busy."

"You heard about the big to-do out at the Delgado's?"

"Sure. Don't affect me none. Buzz off."

"'K, but thought you'd want to hear my other tidbit — some dirt I overheard about you today. If it's floating around my crowd, it's gotta be all over your school by now. But guess you don't care."

Watching these two always made Kendra think of how a cat toys with its prey.

Tyler sighed and hit the Pause button. "Okay, spill."

"You gonna give us a ride when we need it?"

"Dream on." The video game jumped back to life.

"Come on, Kendra." Audrey headed for the door. "He doesn't care that his girlfriend's gonna be a shriek-bitch the next time he sees her."

Tyler hit the joy stick so hard, Kendra thought it might snap. "What the hell you talkin' about?"

"Word's goin' around that you're sweet on that new girl — the one just moved here from Idaho? Heard you were draped around her like slime. Even walked her to class."

"I did not!" His fair skin sprouted mottled red patches on his neck and cheeks.

"Hey, I don't care — I'm just the messenger." She wheeled and walked away, hiding a huge grin. "Don't forget, you owe us a ride now."

As they headed toward the kitchen, she had to ask, even though she knew the answer, "Did you really hear that about Tyler?"

"'Course not, silly. You feel better?"

She had to admit she did. Even witnessing Audrey's mean-ness toward her brother somehow made her feel safer. And her friend was right — she did tend to think the worst was going to happen and worse yet, she wanted to stop it at all costs. Well, she'd take a step back, as of right now.

Chapter 2

Police Chief Deidre Goodwin sped past the recently planted corn fields that fronted the Delgado farm. She slowed the car and turned into the rutted driveway. As the newly promoted head of Finchville's police department, she had plenty to do. *And now this?* She hoped it was just an accident. Even though her exemplary work on the Cloud Nicholson case had earned her this promotion, she didn't need any more killings in her little community. It was unheard of. *'Course, it's an accident. Has to be.*

Steering her cruiser around the deepest ruts of the driveway, she parked next to another black-and-white. As she approached the house, she saw a man sitting on the porch, head in hands. *Husband...what was his name again? Oh yeah, Ricardo.* She didn't want to talk to him. Not yet. She was relieved when she saw Chucky Prescott, her newest addition to the department, barreling towards her. His Adam's apple worked in his throat and his big green eyes were bigger than ever.

"Am I glad to see you, chief!"

"So, what's the deal?"

"Hubby says she was helping him plant, and left to fix their noon meal. He came in a while later and found her. Body's in the hallway by the front door." He waved her around to the front of the house, which faced the road.

She followed his long strides. When she entered, she was almost more shocked by the condition of the hallway than the sight of the body. Boxes were stacked precariously on each side of the hall. They nearly grazed the ceiling. The tiny path that did exist through the cardboard cavern was covered with random items: a hockey stick, a vase with flowers long-dead, a toddler's tricycle, a baseball trophy, and much, much more. The top of a winter boot flopped over into a pool of blood around the woman's head, a reminder of winters past. Of course, she'd heard of hoarders — but man — this was something else.

Glory Delgado lay with her head closest to the door, like she was exiting that way. *Strange.* Farmers didn't normally use their front door. It was more convenient to come and go through the back porch. Even visitors normally used the back. She scratched her head. Maybe she was looking for an item in this mess and something toppled over. As she looked at the chaos, it wasn't hard to see things that could've killed her, if they struck her just right. Or maybe she had a medical condition. She was young — looked to be in her mid-forties — but it happened sometimes.

"Looks like Glory's gone to her glory." Chucky startled her back to the present.

The chief turned and scowled at him. "A little respect for the dead, please." He'd recently graduated from the Nebraska Law Enforcement Training Center in Grand Island. She knew it'd be a while before he'd be comfortable in the job, and he was clearly overexcited. She reminded herself to be patient.

"Yes, but you gotta come around to the back. Now."

"Hold on, Chucky. For cripe's sake, I just got here." She snapped on her latex gloves and took in the flies swarming over the body, like jet airplanes in a holding pattern. One landed on the victim's face and crawled across her chin. Deidre shivered inwardly. She wanted to get down next to the body for a closer look. But there was so much stuff all around the victim, plus that dark pool of blood, which she didn't dare contaminate. And her own girth didn't help. So, she squatted as close to the body as possible, lifting the woman's long raven hair which had fallen across her cheek. There was a lot of blood on her face and head so it was hard to tell, but it appeared there was a deep wound at her temple.

She leaned forward for a scent. She'd seen the actor who played Sherlock Holmes on the TV series, "Elementary," check newly discovered corpses this way, and thought it was really smart of him. So, why not? The smell of sunbaked skin and blood filled her nostrils. But there was something else. *Something faint. A man's cologne.* She extended her hand for her officer to help her upright, then scribbled some quick notes on her pad. "All right, show me."

Together, they tramped around to the back door and passed by the husband, who sat unseeing in an old rocker on the wrap-around porch. "I'll be right with you, Mr. Delgado," she said. There was no reply.

In the kitchen, she was once again overwhelmed. The only clear spot was on the table, and that was barely large enough to assemble a sandwich. Every surface was piled with food, dishes, pans, papers, and unrecognizable items. *How in God's name had this woman cooked?* There were so many nauseating odors, it was overpowering: rotting meat, mold, stale beer, and who knows what else. More flies, plus a trail of large red ants marched across the lip of the sink. A Halloween decoration framed the window. Real cobwebs adorned it. *Well, they've got a jump on next Halloween.*

"Here, this is what I wanted you to see." Chucky pointed to some hair and a dark stain on the corner of the kitchen table.

Sure looks like blood. "Nice catch. You didn't touch anything in here, right?"

He stiffened. "Do I look like an idiot?"

"Didn't say that," she said grumpily. "Get the Nebraska State Crime Lab out here right away. Maybe she just tripped on something in all this mess, but what was she doing in the front hallway if she was supposed to be getting a meal together? We've gotta be sure of cause of death."

"Maybe she was looking for a bandage or something. Obviously, they don't keep things in the normal places in this house," Chucky said as he brought up the number of the Grand Island branch of the state crime lab on his cell.

"Pitching a little sarcasm, huh?" She couldn't help smiling a little. "All right, time to talk to the husband. You got crime tape in your car?"

"You kiddin' me? Parking tickets, yes. Crime tape, no."

"No worries — CSU will have it. In the meantime, look around the barn and out buildings. And make sure no one comes on the property. And Chucky — tread lightly out there."

"Yes, ma'am." He pivoted and headed out the door.

She found Ricardo still motionless in the rocker. His wrists hung limp over the end of the arms of the chair. Not a tall man, he was huskily built with strong facial features. There was no room for her to sit, with more of the same overflowing mess here, so she squeezed herself between the porch rail and the deceased's husband so she could see his face as he talked. "Mr. Delgado?"

His gaze shifted to her from somewhere far away. "Yeah?"

"I'm so sorry for your loss." When she received no response, she paused a minute, then forged ahead. "I know the last thing you want to do right now is talk to me, but I just need a little information. Could you tell me what happened to your wife?"

"Already tol' the young guy."

"Yes, he said you've been very helpful. But do you think you could answer just a couple more questions? I'd appreciate it so much."

He nodded.

"When you came in for your meal and found her, did you try CPR?"

"Nah, her eyes were open and staring straight ahead. Felt her neck. No beat." He spoke in a heavy Mexican accent. "I called nine-one-one."

"Did you touch anything around her?"

"Don' think so."

"That's good. You did exactly the right thing."

A look of relief seemed to pass over his face.

"So, let's back up a little. How long was she at the house before you discovered her?"

"Not sure. Maybe a couple, three hours." He scrubbed his head and his short hair stood in points.

"That's a long time to make a meal, isn't it?"

"You saw the kitchen." Anger rose in his voice. "Takes forever to do anything in that rat's-nest."

"I get your point."

"Knew she'd barely be started and I'd have to help her. Besides all the clutter slowing her down, she gets distracted. And sometimes I come in and just find her sitting there."

"Really? How come?"

"She gets sad." He scrubbed his head so hard this time that she expected to see hair come away in his hands. "We lost our little girl, Sophie, years back. That's when the hoarding started. Thought if we moved out of town, made a fresh start, she'd get better."

"I'm so sorry, Mr. Delgado. I didn't know about your daughter." She closed her notepad and tried to hide her surprise at the news. "Um, do you have somewhere you could stay for a night or two? We need to figure out what happened here."

"But I got livestock needs tending. Cows need herded in and milked...."

"I'm sure someone will help out. Who can you call to come get you?"

"Got a brother in town. Was gonna call him to pick up my boy, Alex, from school. No way can he see his mom like that."

She glanced at her watch. "School bus would already be headed this way, but as soon as it gets here, you and your son can go on into town with your brother. "It'll be fine for him to come out later and do the chores. He just won't be able to go in the house. Better for you to stay in town for now. You're gonna to need some time to work through all this anyway. The farm will probably be the last thing on your mind." She tried to sound reassuring. "Oh, and with your permission, we'd like to keep your truck for a while."

She knew she'd have more questions for him later, but she thought she saw genuine anguish in his eyes. Plus, he'd referred to his wife in the present tense — a likely sign that he hadn't processed the fact she was dead. *Usually means innocence. His interview can wait.*

She left him on the porch and made her way past the fence surrounding the big yard and toward the farm buildings in search of her officer. There was an old-style barn, with its weathered red boards, a chicken coop, a newer pole barn and an equipment shed. She stuck her head in the old barn and saw Chucky moving gingerly around — at least as gingerly as he could. *He's not the most graceful person in confined areas.* "Anything of interest?"

"Not so far. But I'm sure you'll want CSU to look it over."

"Yeah," she replied. "We'll ask them to do the outbuildings first so Delgado's brother can do chores. The house is gonna be a nightmare to go through. I'm not even gonna do my usual inspection. Never seen such a mess. This'll be a breeze in comparison. Hey, you heard anything about them having a little girl who died?"

"Nah. Only know about the boy — middle schooler, I think."

"Huh. Me, either. I told hubby to collect his son and stay somewhere else for a night or two. School bus should be here soon." Her sharp eyes looked around and saw nothing amiss. "Better come out of there before you contaminate something. Go on up and take a peek in his truck without getting in it, or touching the outside. We'll process it later."

She gingerly stepped around the goat and chicken droppings in the barnyard and headed to the pole barn. *Glad it hasn't rained in a while. I hate getting this yucky stuff on my shoes.*

She stepped into the huge metal building. Pigeons startled her as they scattered from the rafters. She stopped to let her eyes adjust to the darkness. The smell of old corn from last year's harvest filled her nose. She took in the combine, livestock slaughter station and sectioned-off area for feed.

A quick look in the equipment shed revealed nothing of interest. She turned and headed back toward the house. *Wanna be here when the boy arrives. Need to see how Delgado interacts with his son. And how the boy is with his dad, too.*

Settling her wide hips into the driver's seat of her squad car, she radioed the office. "Bianca, I'm going to be out here a good while yet. Anything there I should know about?"

"Nope, just a lot of folks calling to see what's goin' on."

"Doesn't take long for word to get around."

"Yeah, snoopy so-and-sos."

"Just play it dumb for now. Hey, see what you can dig up on this family. I think our night crew has been out here for a couple of domestic disturbance calls. And the husband says they had a little girl who died years back." She signed off, leaned her head on the headrest and closed her eyes. *God, I hope this was an accident, but I've got a bad feeling way deep in my gut.*

Chapter 3

It'd only been a day since Glory Delgado died, but it seemed much longer. Maybe that was because Kendra's head had been whirling since she'd found out about it. It'd even been on last night's news out of Lincoln — just a short blurb about a woman dying in a farmhouse near Finchville — cause of death under investigation. But the fact that it was on the news made her wonder. She grabbed the phone by the kitchen table and dialed Johnny's cell.

It went to voice mail. She looked at the clock — 7 a.m. *He should be done with his chores by now.* But Mr. Haskins was a real stickler for getting things right. In fact, she was amazed that Johnny had such a good attitude about his dad's over-the-top demands. No way would she put up with his pickiness. When she'd questioned Johnny about it, he'd said, "Yeah, he can be an a-hole sometimes, but he knows everything there is to know about farming. Where else am I gonna learn it? He says all the small farms are disappearing — we don't like that."

"But he doesn't even want you to play your Fantasy Baseball. Is that fair?"

Johnny had grinned. "Hey, he can't watch me every second — you know I'm in second place already, and the season's just begun."

She knew that was true and Mrs. Haskins was in on the deception. She'd been there one day when Johnny's mom had seen a cloud of dust in the driveway and called a warning to "Close up that laptop!"

Mr. Haskins had stomped into the room and given Johnny the what-for about not bringing the cattle in from the pasture at precisely 4 o'clock.

"I was just headed out," Johnny said, grabbing his Huskers baseball cap. "Can Kendra come along? She rode her bike all the way out here from town."

Mr Haskins gave her a disapproving look. He'd cleared his throat to speak, but before he could say anything, Johnny's mom, said, "Of course, she can. That one heifer is about to pop. Johnny can use an extra set of eyes in case she's gone off from the herd to deliver."

Johnny's dad ran a hand over his face. "Take your cell, and if she's down, call me." He fixed his gaze on Kendra. "And you know not to get anywhere near her, right?"

"Yes, sir." She'd quickly followed Johnny out the door. They'd walked past the barn and begun following the narrow trail beaten down by many hooves. She remembered thinking how cool it would be to see a newborn calf. Even though she'd grown up in Nebraska, she hadn't spent much time on a farm. And there she'd been, on a new adventure, and with the hottest boy ever.

They'd walked for a long time, with the tall grass on the side of the path bending beneath the wind to brush against their legs. Finally, trees began to appear and the trail widened. They reached a stand of poplar and he pulled her over to a fallen log. "Let's rest a minute." She settled beside him and he drew her close. He leaned in to kiss her cheek. She felt like she was falling into nothingness and wrapped her arms around his neck. He moved to her mouth. Behind her closed eyes, a kaleidoscope of vibrant colors and patterns formed and dissolved into new and eye-popping imagery — incredibly random and free — yet secure — that was the way she felt with Johnny.

At that instant, they heard movement behind them. Johnny stood up. "M-m-m-m Boss. M-m-m Bossie," he said in a sing-song voice. Through the trees the herd tramped, huge bodies supported on ankles disproportionately small, full udders swinging, ears pointed to his call. He grabbed her hand. "Let's go." They walked back out to the trail with the creatures following until they were clear of the trees. He stopped and surveyed the herd. "Yup, we're missing Edith."

"Edith? Isn't that a funny name for a cow?"

"Hey, don't look at me. I didn't name her." He shrugged. "Mom's right — she's gone off to do her thing. Gotta find her to make sure she's okay." He tugged her back into the tree grove. She looked over her shoulder and saw some of the cattle were already heading down the trail toward the farm on their own, while others stood and stared after them with their huge brown, long-lashed eyes.

The pair made their way through the trees and across a clearing. A movement caught her eye. "There!" She pointed toward the base of a giant elm.

"Good eyes, Kenny. Let's get a little closer so we can see if she's birthed yet." They crept slowly through the brush until they saw something tiny snuggled against the heifer's side. Johnny pulled his cell out and turned away to call his dad.

She was mesmerized. The baby was a tiny replica of its mother — red with a white face. She was vaguely aware of Johnny telling his dad about the new addition to the herd. She inched closer to see this miracle. Before she could blink, the cow was on her feet and charging. Johnny heard the ruckus and in one motion, jammed his phone in his pocket, ran to her and grabbed her hand. "Come on!" They raced for a nearby tree and he gave her a boost up. The rough bark scraped her hands as she scrambled to the nearest branch with Johnny close behind her. She looked down at the bawling animal and swallowed hard.

"You heard Dad's warning — what were you thinking?"

It was the first time she'd heard anger in his voice. That along with the cow snorting and pawing at the base of the tree made her stomach lurch. "I'm sorry. The baby's so cute — I just wanted to get a closer look."

He settled himself on an opposing branch. "Yeah, forgot you're a city kid." His voice softened a little.

She breathed a little sigh of relief. Another thought made her tense up all over again. "We gonna have to stay up here 'til your dad rescues us?"

"Nah. She'll get it out of her system pretty quick and go back to her calf. And don't worry, I won't tell Dad."

Thinking about that day made her long to be with Johnny again. The morning TV news out of Omaha suddenly snapped her out of her daydream about the newborn calf. *What was the newscaster saying about "Delgado?"* She was amazed to see a picture of the Delgado man fill the screen and tried to grasp what the announcer was saying — something about his wife dying under suspicious circumstances and that the Finchville police were not commenting at this time. "However," the man said, "our investigative reporter has discovered that Mr. Delgado has a criminal record for assault, and served a year here in Omaha at the Douglas County Corrections Facility." His steady gray eyes staring into the camera made Kendra feel like he was talking to her. "Rest assured KETV will continue to bring you the latest on this unfolding story. And now for the weather...."

She was stunned. Johnny had told her that his dad and mom thought there was abuse going on — and now this. *The guy might be a real wacko. And Johnny living right next door. She'd heard countless stories of people going bananas and killing everyone in sight. Geez, she'd even seen her dad in terrible rages that were triggered by the smallest thing — he hadn't killed anybody, but if he'd had a gun, he might've. Got to warn Johnny.* She called out to her little sister, Toni, to hurry and get dressed for daycare.

When she saw Johnny in a crowd of kids outside the school doors, she yelled and waved, and he loped over to her.

"Wanted to call you this morning, but chores took longer than usual. News flash. Mom went over this morning with a casserole, and the place is nothing but yellow tape and cops. She couldn't get anywhere near the place."

"Hey, we gotta talk about this some more. Audrey, too, but she's got some kind of appointment during lunch. Let's meet in the park after school." Then she dropped her bombshell. "Heard on the news this morning that the mister has a criminal record."

"What kind of record?"

Before she could reply, the bell rang and they were forced to run in opposite directions for class. First period flew by, with the rest of the day following suit. Not because she was involved in her classes, but the opposite — her mind swirled with ideas about the case — she knew it was wrong to get involved, but Johnny could be at risk. That meant she had to find out if Mr. Delgado was the killer.

After school, Kendra and Audrey rested their backs against a gigantic oak by the tennis court. Johnny flew down the path toward them and dumped his bike in the grass at their feet.

"Hmm. Bike today huh? Thought you might be on the John Deere," her friend said.

Kendra didn't understand why she had to be so catty to Johnny. Well, maybe in the same circumstances, she'd be jealous, too. She admitted to herself that she did spend a lot of time with him that used to go to her BFF. When she'd first moved here, Audrey was the only one to befriend her. She'd even stuck with her through the whole crazy thing with Grimsby. How many people would do that? Surely, a boyfriend was nothing by comparison. Well, maybe not exactly nothing. She reassured herself by thinking that they'd still be friends when they were tottering about on their walkers in the Happy Valley Retirement Center.

Johnny decided to make light of Audrey's sarcasm. "Yeah, left the tractor parked at the corn crib this time. So, this Delgado stuff is nuts, huh?"

By this time, word had spread through the school about the news that Ricky Delgado had a record, but Kendra excitedly repeated what she'd heard on the news report and how they'd even flashed Delgado's face on the TV screen. She reached out to Johnny, who was lying on his side in the grass. "You could be in super-bad danger. You know that, right? Been thinking about it all day. We gotta do something. Why don't we go check the house out tonight after the cops are gone?"

"OMG, Kendra! You're going off the deep end AGAIN!" Audrey shook her head so hard that her long auburn curls flew against her cheeks.

"Takin' her side on this one — it's a little too crazy, even for me," Johnny said.

She frowned. "Well, okay, how 'bout we just walk by where the husband and kid are staying?"

"What?" It was Audrey's turn to frown.

"Howdja know where they are?" Johnny asked.

"Hey, you forget we live in a town where a secret is good for about ten seconds?" Kendra asked.

"So, where are they?" Audrey replied.

"The brother's house, over on Osborn."

"I don't like the way you're ready to jump in up to your eyeballs all over again," Audrey said. She gave Kendra a nasty look.

"Second that," Johnny agreed.

They began pulling at bits of grass in the awkward silence which followed. There were small white flowers growing amongst it, and as Johnny chewed on a long blade of grass, he wove a little wreath from them. He gently placed it on Kendra's head. "For my princess." He began picking more of the tiny flowers, "And now, one for her lady-in-waiting." He grinned at his own joke.

"Oh, no, you don't!" Audrey exclaimed. She pulled her iPhone from her jacket pocket and began checking her Twitter account.

Johnny followed suit by pulling out his cell. "Scooch over here Kenny. I wanna show you this YouTube video. It's a hoot."

After a while, Kendra saw they were getting bored with their phones. *Here's my chance.* "Whaddup now?"

"No clue," Johnny said.

"Could walk down to the DQ, except no cash," she said.

"Ditto that," Johnny said.

"Well, what then?"

"I know what you're thinking, Kendra Morgan!" Then a look of resignation passed over Audrey's face. "Oh shoot. I know you — you won't give up 'til you get what you want. Let's go then, but we're just strolling by — nothing else, understand?"

She grinned. "'Course. You don't think I'd actually try to talk to them, do you? I'm not totally clueless."

Johnny straddled his bike and worked loops around the girls as they walked along. When they arrived on Osborn, he walked his bike alongside the girls. Reaching their destination, they cast surreptitious glances towards the house. The curtains were closed. No cars in the drive.

"Doesn't look like anyone's there," Johnny said.

"There's a two-car garage," Kendra pointed out. "You don't think they'd actually show their faces to this town of vultures, do you? Probably keeping a low profile."

"I'm sure you're right," Audrey said. "And now that you've seen what you were dying to see, can we go now?"

"Sure," she kept her voice level so they wouldn't know how bummed out she was.

"This is a bust. Hey, let's head back downtown to see if any of the gang is hangin' out," Johnny said.

"'K, but I still think we should go out to the farm tonight. You can sneak out, can't you Johnny?"

"I could. But I'm not." He gave her a shocked look.

"See what I mean? Girl doesn't know when to quit," Audrey said.

Kendra stuck her lips out in a pout. "Guess I'm goin' by myself, then."

"You wouldn't," Johnny said.

"Don't know her like I do," Audrey said to Johnny, then turned to her friend. "But, you're not sucking me in. Anyway, my parents are on high alert after the way we played them on your last 'little adventure.' They'd hear me if I tried to leave. And this is one time I'm happy about that."

Johnny decided to call Kendra's bluff. "Yup, you're goin' by yourself." He jumped on his bike and called back, "Meetcha downtown in a few."

Chapter 4

"It's so dark," Kendra whispered to Johnny as they followed the beam of his flashlight up the long drive to the farm house.

Johnny had called her earlier in the evening. "You're really gonna do it?"

She'd already decided she was too scared to go alone, but his call changed everything. Covering her surprise, she said, "Have to. I need to know what happened to that poor woman. And, your family is a sitting duck."

"Don't think I haven't thought of that? And, Dad, too? The shotgun's locked and loaded. Anyway, what makes you think you know more than the cops?" There'd been no denying the exasperation in his voice.

"Johnny, I know I'm seriously messed up. But don't worry, we won't get caught." She heard a heavy sigh.

"It's a huge mistake, but I can't let you go alone. Meet me by my mailbox at midnight."

Thank God! "Okay — Mom's out like a light way before that — she'll never hear me sneak out. Glad you're coming with me — I'd be so scared by myself."

Now that they were almost there, she felt like her heart was coming out of her chest. She reached out and grabbed Johnny's hand in the darkness. As they drew closer, she saw the yellow tape that circled the house fluttering in the breeze. They ducked beneath it and listened for signs of the dog, Riley. Johnny had warned her about the border collie and how he took his job as watch dog seriously. "They must've taken him into town with them," she said in a trembly voice. A part of her wished the dog was there so they'd be forced to turn back. She swallowed her fear.

The yard light threw eerie shadows as they walked to the back of the two-story house. They pulled on the latex gloves Kendra had found in her mom's cleaning supplies. "Here goes nothing."

They stepped onto the open-air back porch. In the dim light, she made out a narrow pathway to the kitchen door. Making her way through the tight opening, she turned the knob and expected resistance, but the door swung away with a loud creak. Her nose was assaulted with an overpowering smell — rotted something. It sent her stomach into spasms, but she stumbled into the room anyway. "Holy crap!" she exclaimed as Johnny played the flashlight beam over the room. She pulled her own light from her jacket pocket and tried to make sense of the chaos all around her.

Johnny muttered, "This is nuts."

She stared in total disbelief. Finally, her gaze fell on a numbered police marker on the corner of the wooden kitchen table. She saw a dark stain about the size of a quarter. "Look, Johnny. Must be blood." They stood transfixed at the sight until this new shock wore off. "We gotta keep going."

"You insane?"

"We've come this far. Just a quick walk through and we're outta here." She turned and started navigating over and around the mess. Relief flooded her being as she heard Johnny stumbling along behind her, muttering things she was glad she couldn't hear.

As they moved through each room, they found every surface covered with clothing, craft supplies, toys, games, decorations, tools — everything imaginable. Kendra spotted a full bottle of Mr. Clean lying atop a pile of trash and almost laughed at the irony. And everywhere there were plastic shopping bags. Some had stuff in them, some didn't, but it made walking through the place even more like a mine field. And she was afraid to think about the towering boxes stacked willy nilly. If something heavy fell on her, she could meet Mrs. Delgado's fate. There was one room they couldn't enter because it was packed floor to ceiling right up to the doorway. Even the bathroom was jam-packed, including the tub and the sink.

Eventually, they made their way upstairs. The only areas that were livable appeared to be Alex's room and one side of the master bedroom. "This must be Mr. Delgado's side," Kendra said. "Here's a man's watch and some loose change." She pointed to a night stand.

"That confirms the missus was the pack rat," Johnny said.

Her mind was spinning so fast she didn't hear him. She made her way to the other side of the room and pulled open a dresser drawer.

"What're you looking for?"

There was a skittering close by and something ran across her foot. Suppressing the urge to scream, she said, "Anything that tells us more about her."

"We could be here for days and still only know that she was crazy."

She heard the frustration in his voice. "Okay, let's go. But one thing is bothering me. We saw the police marker on the kitchen table that looked like blood, but we haven't seen any sign of where they found the body. They would've marked that for sure. She died in this house, right?"

"Yeah, that's what my folks said, but we've been in every room — the ones we could get into anyway."

She thought for a minute. "Not at the front door." They made their way down the cluttered stairs and to the front of the house, and sure enough, there were yellow markers on the floor and what looked like dried blood. "This is it. Poor thing — she barely had room to fall."

"Can we go now?"

Johnny's shaky voice matched the way her insides felt. "Let's go out the way we came in." Following him slowly to the kitchen, Kendra bumped into a pile of things and it slid to the floor. She shone the flashlight on it, to step safely around, and saw a photo. She picked it up. It had to be a picture of the Delgado family. She recognized Ricardo Delgado from the TV news and she remembered seeing the woman around town — it had to be Glory, and the boy next to her, Alex. But what she found fascinating was that Mrs. Delgado held a little girl in her arms. She looked to be a bit younger than her own sister, who was 4. The toddler grinned into the camera with a mischievous look. Kendra slid the photo into her pocket.

Reaching the kitchen, they heard a car door slam. She didn't need her flashlight to know Johnny's eyes were the size of craters. They were caught. There was no place to hide and no way to run back through the messy house.

The door swung open and a man shone his flashlight into their faces. Kendra could make out the outline of a cop's visored hat. "Don't move," he commanded as he switched on the kitchen light. "Thought I saw a flashlight beam. What in blazes are you kids doing here?"

Kendra breathed a sigh of relief that it wasn't the killer. "I'm sorry. We just wanted to look around."

"Look around! You're in the middle of a crime-scene! I ought to haul you down to the jail and call your parents."

"Oh, you can't. I'd be in a world of hurt," Johnny said.

"Can't, huh?" The man glared at them as he pulled a note pad from his uniform shirt pocket. "Names — and where do you live?" After he learned Johnny lived on the adjacent farm, he seemed to relax some. "So, you were bored and thought you'd snoop around a little, huh?" He eyed the gloves they wore. "Didja touch anything?"

He stepped so close Kendra could smell the stale coffee on his breath. "Not a thing," she lied.

"You will not come anywhere near here again. Understood?"

"Absolutely," she said.

"Now get outta here, before I change my mind. But I'll be reporting this to Chief Goodwin first thing tomorrow morning. I'm sure she'll bring you into the station, so you better be ready to come clean to her, *and* your parents."

She felt his eyes bore into her back as they hurried from the landfill of a house and out into the fresh night air.

Chapter 5

The victim's husband and his son were expected to arrive in Deidre's office any minute. And the crime-scene unit was scheduled to finish processing their farm in a day or two. It'd been a horrific assignment, but the team was doing the best they could. They were photographing everything and dusting for fingerprints wherever possible. The blood and hair samples had been sent to the Omaha lab with a rush request. And a laptop computer found in the home was being checked out.

When Deidre had witnessed Ricardo telling Alex that his mother was dead, she'd noticed nothing suspicious in the man's behavior. As far as she could tell, he was truly devastated, but she still had a lot of questions.

"Hey, chief," Chucky said.

She waved him in. "'Morning. You look kinda ragged — long night?"

"About that. Um." He cleared his throat. "I caught a couple of kids in the Delgado house late last night."

"What?"

"Yeah. Ran 'em off with a warning. Here's their names. The boy lives one farm over." He fumbled a small slip of paper from his shirt pocket.

"Hell's bells, Chucky. Why didn't you call me?"

"Figured you'd be asleep. And they wore gloves, so I didn't think they'd contaminated anything. Not that there's anything uncontaminated in that mess anyway." Defiantly, he crossed his arms.

This is what I get for trusting a new guy. Looking down at the paper he'd thrust at her, one name caught her eye. "Kendra Morgan? A little one, blonde hair?"

"Yup."

She waved her hand in dismissal, not even trying to hide her anger. "Come back after you've gotten some sleep. And Chucky — use your head next time."

She leaned back in her chair and thought about the Morgan girl. *That little twerp. She's up to her old games.*

"Chief, they're here," Bianca's voice interrupted her thoughts. She looked at her receptionist/assistant and her flashy outfit. Her tight magenta top and even tighter mini-skirt made her wonder how she could breathe or sit down. And the woman's hoop earrings looked large enough to circle her neck. *She's flashy, but unlike others I know, at least she follows my instructions.* She caught sight of her visitors standing behind Bianca.

"Have a seat, Mr. Delgado." Deidre motioned to a couple of chairs in front of her.

The man stood uncertainly in the doorway with his hand on his son's shoulder. "Call me Ricky. Can you talk to Alex first so he can leave? He's been through a lot."

"Sure, Ricky."

"And I wanna be here."

"Of course."

He led the boy in and they sat in front of the big desk.

"Hi, Alex. I'm Chief Goodwin, but you can call me Deidre if you want." She smiled at him.

He lifted his head briefly and mumbled a hello.

"I'm so very sorry about your mom. Only have a couple of questions. Then we'll get you out of here."

The boy slumped in the chair and kept his head down. He was small in stature and it seemed he was willing himself to be even smaller.

"Where do you go to school?" Of course, she knew the answer, but she hoped the question would help put him at ease.

"Spencer Middle." The boy's eyes looked everywhere around the room, except at her.

"And what grade are you in?"

"Seventh."

"Can you speak a little louder?"

"I said, 'Seventh.'"

"I understand you have a laptop. What kinds of things do you use it for?"

"Just homework," he muttered. He finally looked directly at her and she saw the pain and confusion in his dark eyes.

"I know this is hard for you, Alex, but you're doing great. Does your dad ever go online?"

"No, never." The boy looked at his dad and Ricky reached out and patted his son's arm.

"Okay, just one more question. Have you ever seen anyone acting suspicious around your mom?"

Alex shook his head.

"How about around you — or your dad — or even the farm?"

"Tha's more than one question," Ricky interrupted.

"I know, but it's important," she said. "Please look at me when you answer, Alex."

Instead, the boy looked at his dad. *Did something pass between them?*

He turned back to her. "No. Haven't seen anyone around. Nobody'd wanna hurt my mom. Everybody liked her."

"You've been a huge help." She rose and shook his small, clammy hand. "Thanks for coming in."

Ricky patted him on the back. "You did good, son. Go on back to Uncle Manny's now."

Now we get down to business. Bianca had unearthed more information about how the Delgado family had lost their toddler six years ago. But Deidre wanted to hear Ricky's version before she moved on to the issue of his temper.

"How long this gonna take?" he asked.

"Not long. Do you mind if I record our conversation?" She pulled a tape recorder from her desk drawer.

"Fine."

"Great. It'll go a lot faster if I don't have to take notes." She pressed the Play button. "Today is April 20, 2013. Present is Ricardo Delgado, also known as Ricky Delgado. Conducting the interview is Chief Deidre Goodwin with the Finchville Police Department, Finchville, Nebraska. Questions are in relation to the death of Mr. Delgado's wife, Glory Delgado."

"Ricky, please start by telling about how you found your wife's body."

He recounted the story as he had told it to her the day of Glory's death.

"I see. And you told me that, due to the condition of the kitchen, it took her a long time to prepare food. And that's why you didn't come in for your meal until two or three hours after she left off helping you with the planting?"

"Yeah."

"How long do you think it was, exactly?"

"Not sure. Usually, she'd go in 'bout eleven and tell me to come in at noon. But I knew she'd be lucky to have it done by one, and that was with me helping. Sometimes, she'd pick up something already cooked at the grocery. That was better. But she was cookin' from scratch that day."

"Understand how you'd prefer the ready-made things. You're working hard out there — a man needs a good, hot meal without waiting so long."

He shifted in his chair. "Yeah. But you don't get it. Wasn't always like this. She used to be great in the kitchen. She hated that it took her so long."

"Yeah, hoarding can really mess things up."

His dark eyes flared with anger. "You judgin' her?"

"Never." She backpedaled. "I'm very sympathetic to what all of you were going through. I'm sorry if I misspoke. Could you tell me how the hoarding began?"

The anger in his eyes changed into the despair she'd seen reflected in his look previously. He nodded and drew a breath. "She was always a saver, but after we lost our little Sophie, things changed. More and more stuff showed up. And nothin' ever, ever got thrown out. Didn't know what to do. Really bothered Alex, too."

"So, it was after you lost your little girl. That must've been so terrible. Tell me about that."

His spine stiffened. "Why? Got nothin' to do with all this."

"Again, I'm sorry, Ricky. Just being thorough — that's all." She used her most reassuring tone.

A huge sigh escaped his barrel chest. "One day Glory had a neighbor in for coffee. Sophie and Alex were playing in the yard with the neighbor's kids. The older ones and Alex were s'posed to be watchin' her. They were playing hide-and-seek — tha's why they didn't notice she was gone. Riley jumped the fence. Damned dog loves to chase cars. She went after him." He rubbed his palms over his jeans. "The truck driver who hit her was a mess. Glory said he couldn't even talk for a while, but he finally told her that first Riley ran out, and then Sophie. No way he could stop in time."

"We were never the same after that. And the house just kept filling up with more and more junk. Thought if we moved to a different town — got a fresh start...."

She saw his faraway look and recognized that the man had traveled to another place in his mind. She rapidly pulled him back to the present. "Did your wife get any therapy for her obsession, Ricky?"

"Oh yeah. And drugs, too."

"What drugs?"

"Um, Paxil. S'posed to help the hoarding thing. Didn't though. Wasn't long before the new place was all filled up, too."

"Sorry to hear that. Can you tell me a little more about your wife? I hear people really liked her."

"Oh yeah, they did. And she liked them, too. Tha's why I felt bad trying to keep her home."

"You wouldn't let her go into town?" Her interest peaked.

"Tried, but it was impossible."

For the first time since she'd met him, his face almost relaxed into a smile. "Every shopkeeper in town was friends with her. Was the only way I knew to keep her from bringing more crap in, but no matter what I said, she couldn't quit shopping."

"I see. Ricky, our records indicate there were domestic disturbance calls."

His near smile morphed to a grimace. "Yeah, sure, we fought. Only 'bout the hoarding. Drove me nuts. How would you like livin' like that?"

"I wouldn't," she admitted.

"Had to fight like the devil just to keep Alex's room clear, and my side of the bedroom. Tol' her lotsa times I'd take the boy and leave. But never could."

"So, tell me about the times we were called out."

"Only twice. Once, I lost it when she came in with a big bag of girl's clothes that were the size Sophie would've been now. Jus' seeing all the soft little-girl colors — it was too much. I grabbed Glory and shook her a little."

"Who called us?"

"She did. Right away she was sorry — called to cancel — but your guys were already on the way."

"And the second time?"

Ricky looked away from her. Even with his dark complexion, she could see the red coming up his neck and into his cheeks. *Is he embarrassed or angry?*

"She charged two hundred bucks for more stuff we didn't need. I went through the roof. Glory never argued with me when she knew I was right, but this time she did. Made me even madder."

"Were you drinking?"

He hesitated. "Just a few beers."

"What happened?"

He looked down in his lap and muttered something in Spanish.

"I need English, Ricky."

"Pushed her against the wall and slapped her."

"Then what?"

"Alex heard the noise and called nine-one-one."

"So, your son knew you were abusing your wife?" She set her jaw.

"Think I'm proud of it? Makes me feel like a low-life."

"So, the CSU found a lot of beer and empty cans. You drink a lot?"

He glared at her. "Livin' like that, wouldn't you?"

She leaned forward and stared into his eyes. "Seems like you're making a lot of excuses. Ricky, did you kill your wife?"

He gulped. "No. I loved her."

"But you've said how you lost your temper with her. Isn't it true that when you came in from the field, and your dinner wasn't ready, you lost it?" She watched him carefully, waiting for an answer. When none came, she pressed on. "I understand perfectly. You were hungry and tired. And for the millionth time, you had to get your own meal. It was finally just too much."

He brushed at his eyes with the backs of his hands. "How can you think that? You tol' me you don't think she died right away. Don' you think I would've called for help if I'd hurt her?"

She had no answer for his question. He was convincing when he said he loved her, but she'd certainly heard of people panicking and doing the wrong thing. She continued to question him about his marriage, and the events on the day of Glory's death. She decided to keep her knowledge of his old criminal offense in Omaha quiet for now, instead trying to give him the option of saying the whole thing was an accident. But, however she framed her questions, he never wavered in his story, and her gut said that in spite of the circumstantial evidence against him, the man was probably innocent. After he'd left her office, she mulled over the interview in her mind. She knew she couldn't rule him out yet. *And there are lots of other possibilities to check out. First thing I'm gonna do though, is shake up that Morgan kid.* She dropped the tape of the interview at Bianca's desk and asked her to enter it in their computer system and print out a hard copy. "I'm headed over to the middle school — be back in a few."

Chapter 6

Kendra pulled her English book from her locker and pushed the door shut. Turning to head down the hall, she saw Mr. Colton, the vice principal, waving his hand above the sea of kids' heads. *He's looking at me!*

"You need to come to the office now!" he yelled over the noise.

Did something bad happen to Mom or Toni? She jostled her way through the mass of kids going to class. When she reached the office, and saw Deidre Goodwin standing at the reception counter with her hands on her hips, her stomach clenched. *That cop ratted us out.*

"Hello, young lady. We need to talk."

She managed a weak response.

"Hear you were at the Delgado place last night."

Heads swiveled at the chief's statement. The normal hubbub of the office came to a standstill. She cringed. Bobby Winston leaned on the counter. *He'll have this news all over school.*

"Naughty, naughty." He grinned.

"Bobby, take your late slip and get to class." Mr. Colton said.

The chief pulled Kendra out of ear shot of the others. "So, what do you think you were doing out there?"

She could see the muscles twitch in her jaw. "Nothing." She looked at her shoes.

"That's not what Officer Prescott says. Told me that you and the Haskins boy were inside the house pretending to be detectives — latex gloves and all."

She was silent in the face of the woman's anger.

"You have no right to insert yourself into this investigation."

"I know. I'm so sorry," she muttered.

"Did you touch anything? You might've contaminated the scene. If you did, I need to know now."

Again, she lied. "No — we just looked around — honest. Won't go near the place again."

"Damn right you won't. Or you'll be payin' your respects to the jail walls."

She knew she'd stepped over the line, but it still hurt to hear this woman she respected so much, rag on her. *And with half the school listening, too. Apparently, helping solve Cloud's case last winter doesn't count for anything.* She watched as Deidre whirled her ample frame, and stomped out of the office. She choked back her tears. *I won't give these people anything more to gossip about.*

After school, Kendra watched Johnny dribble a soccer ball effortlessly to where she sat in the bleachers.

"Hey, waddup? Your mom bust you when you got home last night?"

"No, she works so hard at the café, a semi could roll through and she wouldn't hear it. She has no clue I was gone. But the police chief called me to the office after second period."

"The head of the cop shop?" He looked stricken.

"Yeah. She really reamed me. Can't believe you didn't hear about it — Bobby the Blabber was there."

"Yeah, that Winston kid is a real pain in the butt." Johnny scooped the ball up, put his arm around her, and they walked toward the boys' locker room. "Sorry 'bout that. Must've been a major embarrassment, but you do remember I was against the whole deal?"

"It was stupid of me, I know."

He frowned. "If she calls my folks, Dad will kill me. I hate to think how many extra chores he'll dump on me. He'll ground me, too."

She thought of how she'd felt that day in the pasture with Johnny — how his kiss had made her feel like she was inside a kaleidoscope — all bright and twirly and out of control, yet safe and secure. She brushed her lips lightly at the memory and pushed away the possibility of Johnny being grounded. That would suck big time. "She's just mad at me — she won't call 'em." She knew her words were meant to convince herself as much as they were to calm Johnny.

Chapter 7

"Chucky?"

"Yeah?" He fumbled the car radio to his mouth.

"You're back? Get some chow and sleep?" Deidre asked.

"Yup."

"Don't think this woman's death was an accident."

"Really?"

She heard the surprise in his voice. "Besides gettin' rough with his wife, turns out he got nailed for assault in a bar fight. Served time in Omaha way back when."

"No kiddin'?"

"Yeah, but somethin' seems off. Know he looks good for it, but after quizzing him for a long time and giving him plenty of chances to say it was an accident, he's sticking to his story. 'Course, all bets are off if the lab results show different. For now, we're gonna talk to everyone in town. That's good police work anyway. Don't want anybody saying we rushed to judgment on this guy. So, here's what we're gonna do. The vic liked to shop, so let's start with the stores on Central and talk to every owner. See what else we can find out about her. You take the east side and I'll do the west."

"Roger that."

"Ask lots of questions. Take good notes."

"Yes'm."

"And Chucky? Besides finding out what they've got to say about Mrs. Delgado — ask if they've seen any strangers in town. If this wasn't an accident and it's not the husband, it's hard to believe a local would've done this."

As she headed to Central Avenue, she put a call into Bianca at the office. "Hey, check our records to see if we've picked up any vagrants lately." She could hear the woman snapping her gum over the line. It always set her nerves on edge — today worse than usual.

"Sure thing."

"Call me right away if you find any."

Ignoring the stares of people on the street, she nosed her cruiser into the angled parking and headed into Pearl's Boutique. A little bell tinkled as she entered the shop. The smell of lavender wafted everywhere. "How you doing, Miz Pearl?"

"Why fine, Deidre. How 'bout you?" Without waiting for a reply, the woman said, "Land's sakes! What's the world coming to? Heard that poor Delgado woman was murdered."

The chief and Pearl went way back. Since she was ancient enough to qualify as her grandmother, Diedre never objected to the woman calling her by her first name. She leaned casually against one of the big display cases. "Don't know that for sure — probably an accident — just gettin' all our duckies in a row. So, I hear Mrs. Delgado liked to shop. She come in much?"

"Oh, my achin' back! 'Course she did — in here at least once a week." Pearl patted the grey bun at the nape of her neck. "She'd always find somethin' to buy, too. Even if it was just a trinket."

"So, it's true she went a little overboard on the collecting?"

"Everyone knew she liked to shop, that's for sure. I liked the girl. Never said 'no' to a cup of tea with this old lady."

"Remember when you saw her last?"

"Tuesday morning. Always get my FedEx delivery late Monday afternoon. Could count on her to come in to see what was new."

"How'd she seem?"

"Same as always, I guess. But memory's not what it used to be."

"I'd say it's pretty darned good. Anything else?"

Pearl shook her head and her heavy jowls jiggled. "Nope, just that folks are real scared. This used to be a safe place to live, but with that crazy killer last winter and now this business, nobody knows what to think."

"Yeah, Finchville was safe for a long time. Keep your doors locked, don't you Pearl?"

"I do now. Along with the rest of the town."

"Good. Well, better get going. Lots of people to talk to. Say, you seen anyone around town you don't know?"

Pearl's hand clutched at her sunken chest. "What do you mean? Are you after a stranger?"

She instantly regretted putting Pearl on alert. The last thing she wanted was to frighten the old soul more than she already was. "No. Nothing like that, dear." She gave Pearl a reassuring smile and patted the back of her hand. "I've taken up enough of your time. Thanks for the info and don't you worry now, hear? My officers are patrolling the town 'til we get this thing wrapped up."

The rest of the day passed with much the same outcome as her interview at the boutique. The shopkeepers all confirmed the victim's compulsive shopping and how likeable she was. Nothing useful had surfaced. At five o'clock, she headed back to the office to read her notes onto tape. Chucky had radioed that he was close behind.

"How'd it go?" she called as she heard someone stumble into some furniture and knew it could only be her deputy.

"Nobody was telling me anything we didn't already know 'til I got to The Trading Post. You remember Sam Edelson? Runs the place since his dad passed?"

"Yeah. And?" She leaned forward in her chair.

"Told me that he'd sometimes special-order stuff for her." He relaxed into the chair before Deidre's desk.

"Think they were having an affair?"

"Geez, no. Ever seen the guy? He's uglier than a sow pig rootin' around in the mud."

"What then?"

"Don't know. Probably my imagination, but I felt like he was holdin' somethin' back."

"Like what?" Deidre demanded.

"Honestly don't know. Really, the only thing that was different from everybody else, was the custom orders." He sighed. "Forget it. I'm probably lookin' at people too hard."

She nodded. "Know the feeling. Well, hand over your notes. I'll record them for you — that's if I can read your writing. We'll hit it again in the morning."

The night had been a long and restless one for Deidre. For what seemed the hundredth time, she peered at the digital numbers on the clock. Four a.m. She threw back the covers and walked to the kitchen to brew her coffee. *As long as I'm up, I'll go talk to this Edelson guy. It'll be good to go early — catch him off guard. Maybe Chucky's on to something.*

The man's home was a mid-size pale yellow rambler set on a large lot. There was a bare-bones grass lawn with no sign of flowers or even a shrub. She parked her car and followed the winding sidewalk to the front door. She rang the doorbell. Sounds came from within. No response. She rang again.

Finally, the door opened and a man pulled a threadbare robe around his waist and stared at her through what appeared to be a sleepy fog. A lock of hair hung over one eye. "Police?"

"Mr. Edelson?" She remembered Chucky's comment about the man being ugly. *He's not a knock out, but I've seen worse.* He looked to be in his mid-thirties and stood about six feet tall. A premature paunch showed beneath the robe. There *was* a lot wrong with his face though. *Definitely not a babe magnet.*

"Yeah?"

"Chief Goodwin," she gestured to the badge fastened at her belt. "Sorry to call so early, but we're working on the Glory Delgado case, and manpower is limited. Means long hours for us."

He swung the door wide and held open the screen door for her to pass through. "Mind if I get some slippers?"

She caught the smell of dried sweat. "No problem."

"Have a seat." He gestured toward an overstuffed chair. "Be right back."

She glanced around the room. She'd expected it to be more crowded. Most of the store owners she knew tended to bring home a lot of their own product, but this room was sparse. There was the chair she sat in, a leather sofa, two end tables, and lamps. Some reading glasses and a book were on one of the end tables. A few well-rendered paintings made the room a little more welcoming. And of course, there was the requisite wall-mounted television set – it looked to be a 42 incher.

"How can I help you? Already talked to the young guy yesterday." He perched on one of the arms of the sofa. His hair was slicked back and he suddenly seemed very awake.

"Just wondering what you could tell me about the deceased? Officer Prescott said that she visited your store regularly."

"Yeah, but not just my store. You must know by now she had a disorder."

"Good for business though. You must've loved that."

He gave her a stare. "You're not suggesting I shouldn't have sold to her?"

"Of course not. Just saying. What kinds of things did she buy?"

"Well, I've got everything from tourist items to clothing to antiques. She liked it all."

"My officer said you'd sometimes custom order things for her."

"No, definitely not custom. But if she'd see a dress she liked, and it wasn't the color she wanted, I'd see if some other store in Lincoln or Omaha had it." He tapped his foot on the floor.

She thought he was acting defensive, but she knew that didn't necessarily mean anything. Lots of people got uptight talking to police. "So — she liked clothing?"

"Yeah, most of the clothes she bought were for little girls."

"You know she didn't have a girl, right?"

Edelson rose from the sofa. He pulled the belt of his robe tighter. "Sure."

She continued, "But you sold them to her anyway?"

"She had problems, okay?" His voice rose an octave. "But she was a great human being — I'm sure you've learned that with your investigation. I didn't want to disappoint her. Look, I've gotta open up soon. We finished?"

"All right, Mr. Edelson. Appreciate you talking to me." Deidre rose and headed for the door. "I'll be in touch if I have any other questions," she said as she made her way down the walk.

The only response was the door slamming behind her. Back in her vehicle, she chugged down the last of her coffee from her go-cup and thought about him. She agreed with Chucky. Something seemed hinky about the guy. But hinky was a long way from being a killer.

She called into the office. Bianca said the dump of the Delgado landline and Alex's cell phone hadn't turned up anything unusual. Well, that was her receptionist's opinion. She'd check into that more thoroughly soon, but what she found more intriguing, was the news that there had been a couple of arrests of homeless guys recently. *Better get into the office.*

Chapter 8

Kendra smoothed down the curled edges of the photo she'd taken from the Delgado farmhouse and studied it for the thousandth time. The parents stood side by side with Alex in front of them. A little girl nestled in Glory's arms. They were all dark-skinned, except for Glory. She had dark hair, but her skin shone a gorgeous alabaster white. A happy family? Or did the toddler belong to someone else? She reached out with chubby fingers to whoever was taking the picture. Who was she? Johnny had told her he'd heard that the Delgado family had a little girl, who'd been killed in an accident. They stood by a huge peony bush in full bloom. Springtime. A very different springtime.

She looked again at the picture in the dim light from her bedside lamp and her heart went out to them. Mom and Toni were asleep hours ago, but her mind refused to stop whirling. *I've got to know more about this family, and what happened to Glory. But if I get caught, the chief will be even madder at me.* She made up her mind. *I've gotta chance it. Should I sneak to the phone and call Johnny? No, too risky. He'd made it clear he wouldn't be caught up in her games ever again.*

She slipped into her capris and shirt. Jamming her feet into her tennies, she tiptoed to the window with jacket in hand. The full moon cast shadows across the room as she switched off her lamp. She dropped to the ground from the window and crept around the corner of the building. All was quiet in the ten-unit complex.

She unlocked her old Schwinn from the bike rack and walked it to the street. The night air was warm and heavy and seemed to wrap itself around her like a blanket. She knew she should be afraid, sneaking off like this. But she wasn't. Instead a thrill traveled along her spine. She mounted her bike, leaned forward and pedaled as hard as she could. A dog she recognized from one of the houses across the street loped quietly along beside her. When he tired and dropped back, she was sorry to lose his company. She pedaled harder.

Nearing the edge of town, the pavement turned to dirt and the deep ruts carved from last winter's snows threatened to bring her down. She got off and walked the rest of the way to the county highway where she could ride again. She passed one of the huge irrigation units, its shadow throwing an image like a long, prehistoric dragon across the field. She shivered in spite of herself. It was still a few miles to the turn-off and a single lane road to the Delgado farm. *Maybe I am a little scared.*

Suddenly, headlights came over the rise toward her. Dipping down into the ditch by the road, she dropped the bike and flattened herself against the ground. In a flash, the car sped by. She jumped up and felt a stinging in her leg. *Damned cockleburs.* She knew better than to try to pick them out with her bare hands — she'd only end up with them in both body parts. Shakily, she pushed the Schwinn back onto the road and continued on.

After that, with the exception of a huge swarm of fireflies and an owl flapping directly over her, she rode alone. The smell of the spring earth replenishing itself filled her nose. Her heart thumped from the exertion and excitement. She passed Johnny's farm and knew she was close. As she approached the Delgado farm, she could see the outline of the trees providing a windbreak at the northwest side of the property. There were three yard lights — one at the house, one by the barn, and one on a tall pole between the two buildings.

Were *Alex and his dad back?* She left her bike in the grass by the mailbox and walked quietly up the driveway. The yellow tape was gone. *Yup, they're probably here.*

The full moon was bright enough that she didn't need her flashlight. She reached into her pocket and grasped it anyway. She realized her teeth were chattering. *If I have one bit of sense, I'll leave. But I'll hate myself in the morning.* She felt like one of those cartoons with an angel and devil on each shoulder, tearing her apart with their incessant chatter. She took some deep breaths. *Okay, I'll just take one quick look around the barn.* She stepped around to a side door. Swinging it open, she peered into the darkness and waited. As her eyes adjusted, she could make out horses in their stalls shifting occasionally from side to side. Fear threatened to overtake her again. But her ears picked up the gentle lowing of the cattle in their pen outside. She stood and listened to them for a moment. Their peaceful sounds drifted through the night and calmed her jittery nerves.

She switched on her flashlight and walked around inside the barn looking for anything strange. Nothing. Only animal feed, farm tools, and horses. *What did you think you'd find in a barn, you dummy?* She stumbled over a shovel leaned against a work bench. The horses watched her with their huge eyes like they knew she was doing something wrong. She played the beam of the light upward into the hayloft. *I don't want to go up there.* Her feet walked toward it anyway.

She clenched the flashlight in her mouth and climbed the ladder. Her jaw began to quiver. *Don't drop the light.* She didn't like this loft — it was a place where bad things might've happened. Reaching the top, she could make out bales of hay everywhere, a baling hook buried in one of them. *That would make a good murder weapon.* She set her jaw and pulled herself from the top rung of the ladder onto the dusty floor. Tiny feet scurried somewhere. No doubt a rat. *I hate those things!* She forced herself forward, the light shaking so badly now that she gripped it with both hands. Something darker than hay caught her eye. *What was it?* She tiptoed closer, her heart hammering through her chest.

Relief cascaded through her as she realized that it was a sleeping bag — and thank God, it was empty. A soda can and some food wrappers lay beside it. And cigarette butts. *How stupid to smoke in this fire trap. Was it the killer?* She clambered down the ladder on rubbery legs and hurried away.

Riding home, she had more questions than ever. *Why was the sleeping bag there? Surely the cops would've searched the barn from the tip of the weather vane to the floor boards. It must mean whoever was hanging out in the loft was there after the crime-scene unit was. In that case, maybe it's no big deal. Did she dare tell anyone?*

She climbed back through her window and into the safety of her bed. An endless loop of possible scenarios for Glory's death tortured her tired mind. Dawn was beginning to seep through the curtains before sleep finally overtook her.

Chapter 9

Deidre scratched her head with her pencil, her mind miles away from where she sat at her office desk. She agreed with Chucky that Sam Edelson seemed off somehow. But she dealt in facts and there was nothing specific pointing toward the guy.

With police work, everyone connected with the victim had to be checked out. So far, she hadn't totally eliminated anyone, except Manuel Delgado, Ricky's brother. It'd been confirmed by his boss and several of his co-workers that he was at work the entire day of the victim's death.

A further check into the two vagrant arrests was now on her to-do-list. One of the men had apparently left town on the freight train that passed through Finchville. That was, if she could believe the rumors around town. Next step was to confirm that. She grabbed her keys and headed for the homeless camp down by the river. She'd instructed Bianca to fax the man's physical description — big, balding, no full name, nickname, Spike — to all the police stations along the train route.

She parked her car along the gravel road, and descended through the tall trees to the makeshift camp. She walked along, stopping at each tent, jeri-rigged tarp or cardboard home. Each person, who was coherent enough to talk, said they stayed away from this Spike character. They all agreed he was a mean dude.

At the river's edge, she found one last man. He was crouched in front of his tent, breaking up sticks for what appeared to be kindling.

She sat on a log opposite him. "Hi, how's it going?"

"All right."

"I'm trying to find out about Spike. Do you know where he is?"

The man swallowed. "No, hope he's gone though."

"You look nervous. What's going on? He hurt you?"

"Nah, nothin' like that."

"What then?"

He rolled his eyes. "Aren't goin' leave 'til I spill, are 'ya?"

"Nope."

He shook his head. "Few days back, I saw him torture and kill one of the stray dogs that hang around for scraps. Would've stuck my nose in, but he's a strong SOB. Didn't wanna end up like that mutt."

She looked up from her notepad. "Would you be willing to come into the office and make a statement?" A veil fell over the man's eyes and she knew the answer to her question.

"Hey, don't worry about it. You've been very helpful already." She got the man's name and rose from her perch on the log. She scaled the little ravine to her cruiser, the rocks and dirt falling away beneath her boots. *Gotta find that guy. Sounds like a viable suspect.*

The other person of interest, a man by the name of Tyson, had remained around town. In fact, he'd recently spent a night at the jail for public intoxication. She sent Chucky and another officer to re-check the homeless camp.

An hour later, her phone rang. "He's not here," Chucky said.

"Okay, do a town sweep."

It didn't take them long to find him sleeping in the alley behind The Corner Tavern and they happily escorted him into Deidre's office.

She was instantly assaulted with the sour smell of sweat and booze. She rose and opened the window behind her desk and took a gulp of the fresh air, then reluctantly returned to her chair. "Mr. Tyson, I'd like to talk to you about our investigation into the Delgado case."

"The what?" He looked shocked.

"The murder of Glory Delgado."

"You're kidding!"

"She was found dead in her farmhouse right after you were released from our fine accommodations here." She spread her palms.

"I heard about that, but I ain't got nothin' to do with it!" His bleary eyes widened.

"Sure about that? We checked your record — several felonies for breaking-and-entering and aggravated assault make you look pretty fine for this. Doesn't look good for you. Gonna have to hold you 'til you come up with an alibi."

"You can't do that. Got health problems," he whined.

She noted the man's yellowing of the eyes, and the tremor in his hands. She'd seen enough of the symptoms of substance abuse to know this guy was far down the road in his addiction. "You find a doctor who'll say you're at death's door, and we'll see about that. In the meantime, you're once again our guest." Ignoring the look of desperation in his eyes, she yelled through the door for Chucky to collect the prisoner.

Chapter 10

Kendra plodded along behind Toni toward Little Rabbit Day Care.

"Hurry, Ken'ra. Wanna play with Emma. We got dollies with the same dress." Toni skipped along with her doll clutched to her chest.

Usually she was the one urging her little sister to speed it up, but three hours of sleep night before last, and six last night, had her feeling like she was wading through three feet of water. She still hadn't told Johnny or Audrey about sneaking into the Delgado barn. *I need to get this off my chest, but anyone I tell is going to yell at me. And they're right. I've got no business getting mixed up in this.*

What about Peg or Mr. Campbell? They were her only two adult friends. She'd met them when she was trying to uncover who'd killed her friend, Cloud. *Nope. They were hopping mad at me when they found out how I'd manipulated them. They'd tell Mom for sure.*

And I sure don't want to mess things up at home. It's so much better now. That was one of the really great things that had come out of meeting Peg. She and Mom had become good friends and she'd helped Mom grow a backbone. Up until then, their family had been on a continuous move from place to place, trying to stay one step ahead of Dad and his anger. She'd lost track of the number of towns and run-down apartments they'd lived in.

She thought back to the last time she'd seen her dad.

One evening they'd been watching one of Mom's game shows when Kendra saw her tense up. Teresa muted the TV and put her finger to her lips. Toni got a puzzled look on her face, but for once, stayed quiet. Someone was coming unsteadily down the hall. Her mom tiptoed to the door and looked out the peep hole. She didn't answer the loud knock, but slipped away from the door.

More pounding. Dan Morgan yelled, "Let me in! Dammit!"

Her mom fumbled for the phone. "I'm calling Peg," she mouthed.

Kendra heard her whisper into the receiver, "He's here." Whatever Peg said, it was short and Teresa clicked off. She stared into space, with a bewildered look.

The knocking continued and the door rattled in its frame. Teresa called out that she didn't want to see him when he was drunk.

"You'll see me whether you want to or not," he bellowed.

Kendra watched in horror as he kicked in the flimsy door and staggered in. She glanced over at Toni, who cowered in the corner of the sofa, clutching her stuffed dog. He towered over her mom and pulled her to him with a grin. He bent to kiss her on the mouth, but it ended up on her cheek as she struggled to pull free. "Whatsa matter? Don' love me anymore?"

"What do you want, Dan?"

"Just a little sugar. And a drink if ya got it." He stroked Teresa's arms.

She took a step back. "You know I don't keep alcohol in the house."

Kendra thought her mom looked like she wanted to spit in his face.

"Since when?" He pushed her aside and headed for the kitchen.

"Get out!" Teresa was on his heels.

He whirled and smacked her so hard across the face that she crashed into the wall.

Kendra started to go to her sister to comfort her, but something broke in her — a hot rage started at the top of her head and sped through her body. She ran across the room and hurled herself onto Dad's back, grabbing hold of his shirt.

He yanked her off and threw her to the floor like a rag doll. She was vaguely aware of his shirt buttons flying in different directions and the heavy stench of whiskey.

"Why, you little bitch!" His hand went to his belt buckle. "You need a lesson."

Her mind traveled back in time to previous beatings. She'd never given him the pleasure of letting him know the pain she felt. She knew he hated it when she wouldn't cry. It'd been her only revenge. *This time will be no different.*

But now Teresa was back on her feet and moving to put herself between them. "Calm down, Dan. I'll go next door and see if they've got some wine or something." She looked around for her purse. "Kendra, take your sister to your bedroom, right now."

What was going on? Was Mom trying to buy time? Wordlessly, she picked up a sobbing Toni from the sofa and stumbled away.

"Tha's better," Dan slurred, and fell into a chair.

She sat on her bed and tried to steady her voice. Her heart clattered in her chest. "Wanna hear a story?"

"I'm scared, Ken'ra," Toni said, snuggling into her side.

"I know, but we're okay. Not to worry." She wiped away her sister's tears and tried to hide her own fear. "Remember the story about Cinderella?" She launched into the fairy tale, hoping help would arrive soon.

A few minutes later, she heard Mom's voice. *Hopefully she's back with something to keep Dad happy.* Time seemed to drag. Finally, she thought she heard a deeper voice than her dad's. She peeked through her bedroom door and saw two very large men looking at Mom through the doorway.

"Understand you've got some trouble here, ma'am," the stranger said. He had a tattoo sprouting from the neck of his T-shirt and snaking through his buzz cut.

She stared in amazement. The other one reminded her of The Hulk, he was so ripped. She'd overheard Peg assuring Teresa that if her ex-husband knew she had backup muscle, he'd stop the harassment. But she had no idea Peg was going to supply that muscle.

Through the crack in her door, she watched the men grab her dad underneath the armpits and haul him from the apartment

like a ten-pound sack of potatoes. Teresa came in the bedroom and sat stiffly on the bed with them. They listened to
the sounds of thumps and muffled cries outside the window
and could only guess at what was occurring. Whatever it was,
it wasn't good for Dad.

"What's happening?" Toni asked, her blue eyes huge with
wonder.

Teresa broke from her trance. "Nothing for you to worry
about, honey. Let's get you ready for bed." She smiled nervously over at Kendra. "I think everything's going to be much
better now."

And Mom and Peg had been right. Since that night, they
hadn't heard a word from Dad. Rumor around town was that
he'd headed to Utah. And her mom looked happy for the first
time in ages.

Of course, it was hard to get by with no money help
from him. But that was nothing new. Mom still had to
work long hours just to squeak by and that meant she still
had to help out a ton with Toni and the chores, but that
was just fine.

Saying goodbye to Toni in the hallway of the daycare, she
headed off to her meeting place with Audrey where they always
finished the walk to school together. A few blocks from the
parking lot, they saw Johnny jogging toward them.

"Hey," he called. "Ready for another fun day of learnin'?"

Kendra knew he was kidding. Schoolwork was hardly
something he loved, and she agreed with him. It was the
social part that kept them showing up every day. Audrey was

a different animal, though. A real nerd. She doubted she'd ever pulled a B grade in her life.

Johnny fell in beside them, slipping her hand into his big, farm-worn one.

She only wanted to take pleasure in his touch, but told herself it's now or never. "Got a news flash for you guys."

"Oh yeah?" Johnny asked.

"I went out to the Delgado farm again a couple nights ago." She watched Johnny for a reaction. His hand fell away and he stopped in his tracks.

"Did you say 'again'?" Audrey asked.

"Kendra, you promised me!" Johnny interrupted.

Both of them frowned at her. Her BFF placed her hands on her hips.

Johnny looked at Audrey. "Yup, I actually was fool enough to go with her the first time."

"And you never told me?" Audrey's voice had hurt running through it.

"Well, it sounded like you couldn't sneak out of the house, even if you wanted to," Johnny said.

"Still coulda told me about it."

"You'll be glad to know you didn't come with us, 'cuz a cop caught us out there." He turned a withering stare back to Kendra. "After we got busted, you promised me you'd forget the whole mess. Guess your word doesn't mean much."

"So sorry, you guys. I just looked around the barn, okay?"

"No, not okay!" Johnny and Audrey said almost simultaneously.

"But wait 'til you hear what I found."

Johnny rolled his eyes and Audrey looked ready to explode. She whirled and marched ahead, clearly not wanting to know anymore.

She gave Johnny a quick rundown about the sleeping bag and other items in the hayloft, talking loud enough for Audrey to hear. "So, whadya you think?"

Her friend walked faster and didn't turn to answer, but Johnny reluctantly agreed that the sleeping bag was probably left there after the cops had checked over the place. "From what I've heard about Mrs. Delgado, she had a kind heart. Maybe the guys riding the rails knew that and made a habit of stopping there for handouts."

His comment sparked something in Kendra's brain. "But wait a minute. What if a homeless guy killed her, got scared and left? And came back after all the hullabaloo died down?"

"Possible," Johnny said. "Hey — you're not trying to suck us into breaking the law again, are you?"

"No, I just needed to get this off my chest. Hate keeping secrets from my friends."

She could feel the tension running down Johnny's arm as she grabbed his hand.

He pulled away. "I'm serious, girl. You gotta stop this."

"I know. I'm gonna forget all about it. Honest."

Johnny turned and marched away. She could see Audrey already climbing the school steps in a huff, and hoped with all her might that she wasn't losing two of the most important people in the world to her.

Chapter 11

So much for minding my own business, Kendra thought. She'd really meant it when she'd promised to forget about the Delgado woman's death, but she hadn't counted on what she was now overhearing from the two boys sitting behind her in Study Hall.

"Dad says they're holding a homeless dude for the murder," one boy whispered.

"No kiddin'? How does he know?" the other boy asked.

"He's got a friend who works at the cop shop."

"Wow!" the second boy replied.

Is this just gossip? Can't take a chance. The cops need to know about the sleeping bag I saw in the barn. But how can I tell them without getting myself in more trouble? Finally, a light flickered on in her brain.

The last bell rang, and she ran as fast as she could, her backpack bouncing against her spine, toward the public bus stop. She had to hurry or she'd be late picking up Toni from daycare. She rummaged for the proper change and craned her neck for the bus. She took it as a good sign when it creaked to a stop in front of her a few minutes later. She'd seen a bank of pay phones at the shopping mall. The crime shows on TV all claimed that calls could be traced, so she needed to be far away from school and home.

The rocking of the bus made her feel queasy. She pulled the cord to signal the driver she wanted off, when she saw the mall loom into view. Hurrying to the phone bank, she was relieved to see no one else there. Her hand shook as she dropped the coins in.

"Finchville Police Department." A female voice came over the line.

"Uh, hi. I have a tip in the Delgado case." She tried to sound calm.

"All right. I'll transfer you to Chief Goodwin's desk."

"No!" she spluttered. *I thought Deidre would have someone taking messages.*

"Why not?"

"I-I-I changed my mind." She reached to hang up.

"By law, if you know something, you must report it." Whoever she was talking with sounded very stern. "The chief isn't at her desk. But leave a voice mail with your information, and a number where you can be reached. And don't hang up the second I transfer you!"

Struggling with the need to do what was right, and possibly getting herself in more trouble with Deidre, she clenched her jaw. The greeting came on and she couldn't force her hand to place the phone in the cradle. She yanked a tissue from her pocket, and stretched it over the receiver. In the highest falsetto she could muster, she said, "You should look into the Delgado woman helping out homeless — not just feeding them — but letting them sleep in the barn. You need to check out the hayloft." She slammed the phone down and ran for the bus stop.

When Deidre heard the message, she shook her head. Then played it back twice more. The caller was young and even though she was obviously trying to disguise her voice, it sounded familiar. *Oh damn. It's that Morgan kid.* She started to yell out to Bianca to get the girl's mom on the phone, but suddenly stopped. *I hate to admit it, but the girl may've uncovered something. Better check it out first. I'll call Mrs. Morgan later.*

Instead, she punched in Ricky Delgado's number. "Did your wife ever give handouts to homeless folks?"

He cleared his throat. "Yeah. Tol' her not to, but she always said it was a sin not to share the good stuff we raised. That what got her killed?"

"No idea, but there's a possibility someone was staying in your barn."

"Wouldn't surprise me."

"You should've shared that information with me, Ricky."

"Sorry, still tryin' to get a hold on what happened."

"Yeah, it's a lot to take in. We'll check it out."

"Any results from the DNA on the kitchen table yet?"

She listened carefully for any sound in his voice that might betray guilt, but heard only genuine curiosity. She'd pretty much ruled him out, but reminded herself that some killers were very clever. *Maybe he got fed up with her ruining their credit, not to mention the hoarding thing.* "No. I'll call you as soon as I do. I need to look into this latest lead right now. Talk later, Ricky."

"Bianca, where's Chucky?" The woman wobbled in on her stilettos at the sound of her boss's voice. Deidre couldn't help but think that she looked like a Christmas tree about to topple. *Her plump pear shape just isn't meant for those shoes. But they do match her personality. Glam all the way.* She smiled inwardly. *Her efficiency continues to amaze me. Guess it's true — you can't judge a book by its cover.*

"He had a dentist appointment — should be about done," Bianca replied, and blew a huge bubble, then popped it before it could land on her nose.

"You ever consider that bubble gum might not be the best thing for *your* teeth?"

Ignoring her boss's question, she pivoted with surprising grace and left the room.

Deidre picked up her phone and called her officer.

"Yeah, chief?"

"Get your butt out to the Delgado place. Check out the hayloft. If you find anything, don't touch it and call me right away."

"Um, boss? Jus' got done with Doc Jones. Don' know if I should be drivin'. Dentists scare the beejeebers outta me. Gave me a hefty dose of that gas stuff."

She could hear the slur in his words. "Stay right there. I'll pick you up in five minutes." Pulling up to the curb across the street from the dentist's office, she watched Chucky push through the door onto the street.

He saw the cruiser and gave her a wave. Starting into the crosswalk, he at first looked like the agile tight end he'd played in high school football, but when he saw a woman crossing toward him, his feet tangled. He went down. Hard. His long body sprawled every which way. Drivers stopped and gawked. The woman ran forward and helped him up. Deidre looked on in surprise as he wobbled the rest of the way to the car.

"Sorry, Chief!" he exclaimed as he brushed at his uniform and clambered into the car. Nitrous oxide. Works good. Might've had a Diazepam or three 'fore I went in, too."

"I'd better take you home," she said, shaking her head.

"Nah. I'll be fine. Think that woman back there thought I'd been nippin' on the Jack Daniels, though." He giggled.

She knew she should drop him at home to sleep it off, but she was in a hurry to get to the Delgado farm. Plus, she knew it would be a challenge to get her wide body up the narrow ladder into the hayloft. She swung by Mickey D's and ordered a large coffee in the drive thru. "Drink this down." She hoped the caffeine would kick in before they got to the farm.

By the time they got there, he seemed more like himself. She hurried to the house to tell Mr. Delgado they'd be in the barn, but no one answered her knock. Back at the cruiser, she collected some yellow crime tape, just in case.

They found the outbuildings empty, including the barn. She spotted a cloud of dust to the north. *Delgado's probably out in the field. We'll leave him a note if he's not here when we're finished.*

"Okay, up you go," she said gesturing toward the ladder.

Chucky walked a credibly straight line and stood in the beam of sunshine that fell on the floor from the hayloft.

She handed him his latex gloves and gave him a once over while he stretched them over his big hands. *I think he's okay.*

Two over two, up he went, 'til he was almost to the opening. It happened so fast her mouth fell open. Suddenly he was hanging onto the ladder with both hands as his feet dangled beneath him.

"Chucky!" she yelled.

He began pummeling his feet like he was in a sprint. Finally, one foot caught a rung, and then the other. "No sweat, boss. Everything's cool."

She held her hands to her chest and watched as he hoisted himself into the loft. All she could see were his size twelve shoes protruding over the opening. "Pull yourself together, Prescott!" she yelled.

"Aye, aye, Boss!"

"Get away from the edge before you stand up. Then tell me what you see." She knew she wasn't really mad at Chucky, but at herself for gaining so much weight that she couldn't get up that damned ladder — but she wasn't about to tell him that.

"You're right. There's squatter's stuff up here," he called down.

"Okay, don't touch anything. Just take pictures with your phone. I'll call the Grand Island Crime Unit and get them here ASAP. We'll yellow tape up there so Delgado can still milk his cows and feed the livestock. I know the unit checked out the loft at the time of her death, so it's not likely it's anything, but we better get it checked out. Think you can get down here without breaking your neck?"

They left a note taped to Ricky Delgado's door and headed back to town. Dropping Chucky at home, she told him she'd send another officer to pick up his squad car at the dentist's office. "No more driving for you today, young man."

Back at the station, she pulled her keys to the jail and hurried to Jared Tyson's cell. After twenty minutes of re-interrogating her homeless suspect, he insisted he hadn't been at the Delgado farm. He still gave off a rank odor, but after being in lock up, he was now lucid, and she believed he was being honest.

Shoot! With this extra request for processing the stuff in the loft, I bet the lab will take even longer to get us their results. With her mind spinning, her plan to call the Morgan kid's mom had vanished.

Chapter 12

Kendra tried her best to forget about the murder, but the photo of the Delgado family kept haunting her. She'd studied it so much it was imprinted on her brain. In the picture, Alex looked happy. Before all this happened, she hadn't even been aware of his existence, but now that she knew who he was, she kept her eye out for him. When she did catch a glimpse of him at school, he looked lost. She never saw him with any other kids, except at the table in the lunch room with the other outcasts — the overweight ones — the special needs kids — the ones that didn't dress right. With bullying being a big issue, she didn't think any of them were mistreated. Unless getting the cold shoulder was bullying — deep down she knew it was — she'd spent enough time on the fringes, changing schools like some kids changed their clothes. In each new place, she was always ignored at first — it was like she was invisible. Sometimes, eventually, some kid would risk the wrath of their clique by reaching out, but it was always hell suffering through the judgmental stares and sarcastic remarks. Yeah, she could relate.

As she'd watched from a distance in the lunchroom, she noticed Alex didn't even mix with any of the kids at his table.

He just sat hunched over his food, head down, shoulders rolled forward. It made her sad.

Then last Saturday, Mom had sent her to the store to pick up yogurt and cereal, and there he was, standing by the dairy case. "Hi, Alex."

His eyes widened. "Who are you?"

"Oh, I'm friends with Johnny Haskins — your neighbor. He told me about your mom — so sorry." A stormy look came over his face and she knew she'd put her foot in it. "Shopping with your dad?" she asked, trying to save the conversation.

"Gotta go." He shuffled off.

You are such a dummy, Kendra. Do you always have to jabber away without thinking? She'd caught a whiff of strong body odor as he left. *That can't help his popularity at school.* She remembered the night she and Johnny had broken in, and how the bathroom had been as disastrous as the rest of the house. The shower was jammed full of junk. If Alex wanted to clean up, he probably had to do it in the barn where the milking equipment was washed. The whole idea of this dirty kid and his filthy house grossed her out. Then she thought about the look in his eyes. There was so much pain there. *I do feel bad for him.*

Chapter 13

Deidre tugged at her chin and tried to analyze the case while her receptionist fluttered around her. "*What* are you doing?"

"Just straightening up. Looks like you haven't filed anything in a hundred years," she said, clicking her gum.

"Think you could do that later? Trying to solve a murder here."

Bianca's spine stiffened. "Sure, no problem."

Didn't make any brownie points there. But the sound of the woman's stiletto heels tapping out of her office and down the tiled hallway prompted a sigh of relief. The news was bad from the Omaha lab. The DNA results didn't match either of the vagrants. She had really been hoping for a match to Spike, aka Marvin Fogleby, who'd been apprehended in North Platte a few days back.

She tried to console herself with the one semi-positive development. The lab had found an unknown DNA sample in the farmhouse. And it was in the front hallway, which was rarely used. The problem was that they'd run it against all stored samples in CODIS, the national crime database, and come up with nothing. *Probably the killer, but how to find him? Or her? We've re-interviewed everyone who knew Glory, which is basically the whole town. Even double-checked to be sure Alex was in school at the time of the murder. Felt wrong even considering him — but, hey — stranger things have happened. Kids from dysfunctional homes can sometimes shock the daylights out of you.*

I was hoping to spot someone acting weird at the funeral, but no luck there either. Deidre recalled how the sanctuary of St. Mary's had been packed. The only thing that had piqued her interest was that none of Glory's family attended. No mom, dad or siblings. When she'd followed up the next day, she'd learned the victim was an only child and her parents had been dead a number of years. *Maybe that explains why she took to hoarding after their little girl died. A person needs family support during tragedies. And with the exception of Ricky's brother, all of his family's in Mexico.*

She pulled at her chin again. *Got no choice but to play my trump card. Hate like hell to do it, but I've exhausted every other possibility.* She headed out the door to Sadie's Café, calling for Chucky to join her. "Lunch is on me today, my man."

On the walk there, she said "Gonna stir the pot — just go along with whatever I say."

The small café was about half full. *Good. Everyone will be able to hear me.* She slid into a booth at the center of the room and Chucky sat opposite her.

The owner, Sadie Zimmer, rushed over with two ceramic mugs and coffee pot in hand. "Hi, chief. Coffee?"

"Sure. Make that a couple burgers, too."

"Everything on 'em?" Sadie asked.

"That special sauce of yours, no onions," Chucky said.

"Same for me. Fries come with that too, right?"

"Does the sun come up in the morning?" Sadie asked.

"Put a piece of that homemade lemon meringue pie on the tab, too," Deidre said.

Sadie looked at Chucky. "Pie for you?"

"No thanks." He patted his mid-section.

As Sadie walked away, Deidre whispered to her officer, "Here we go. Remember, just play along." She raised her voice and said, "Well, I'm totally out of leads on the Delgado case."

The hum of conversation and clinking of silverware stopped. Sadie froze in her tracks between the counter and the kitchen. She spun around. "What? Nothing on the DNA?"

It never ceased to amaze her that no matter how hard they tried, some classified information always got out to the public. She wondered who'd leaked the fact that the crime lab was checking DNA. But, this time she was happy for someone's loose lips. Made this scene a whole lot easier. She stirred a good amount of sugar into her coffee. "That's right."

"Wow. I thought for sure it'd be a match to that homeless guy you're holding," Sadie said.

"As of five minutes ago, not holding him anymore," Deidre said.

A grizzled man in the booth behind her piped up, "Didn't I hear there was another guy like that you were tryin' to track down?"

"Yeah. With his record, he looked really good for it, but his DNA didn't match either." She shook her head. "Unfortunately, we've still got a murderer out there."

The look of shock on Chucky's face almost made her laugh. She remembered how many times she'd preached to him about not revealing case details, and to *never ever* do anything to spread fear in the community. She'd broken both of her cardinal rules, and to the extreme. She frowned a little at him so he'd remember to play it cool.

A few more folks chimed in with questions and comments, but nothing of help. She was hoping she hadn't screwed up big time by frightening people more than they already were, when a man in a booth close to the door spoke up. "Well, I've heard talk some folks aren't happy to see a Mexican makin' a go of it."

Deidre craned her neck for a look at the man and recognized him as a farmer with a spread west of town. "That right?"

"Yeah. 'Course I got nothing against 'em myself." He looked down at his plate.

A race thing. Why didn't I think of that? Glory was white and married to a Latino. That could ruffle some of the extremely conservative feathers around here. And a lot of folks thought they'd settled this prairie, and didn't like any outsiders, period. She could hardly wait to get going on this new lead. "Sadie, think you could get those burgers in the works? And make it 'To Go'."

"Sorry." Sadie ran for the kitchen. Deidre knew she'd be blathering to the cook about the lack of leads as she gave him their lunch order. "So, anyone specific who doesn't like Mexicans?" she asked the farmer.

"Not that I know of," he replied.

"Give me your name and number, sir. We may need to talk with you later."

"So now what do we do?" Chucky asked when they were back in Deidre's office. The smell of their burgers attracted Bianca to the door.

Deidre piled a handful of fries on a napkin and held them out to her. "We wait. I'm hoping it won't be long before some new tips come in. In the meantime, we think about people we've heard make racial slurs."

They'd barely finished their lunch, when the farmer from the café appeared. "Uh, I've got a little more info, but didn't want to say back there." He motioned over his shoulder.

"I understand. Tell me," Deidre said.

"Robert O'Connor. He's got that big acreage not far from mine. Says he don't mind Mexicans helpin' out with the harvest, but doesn't see why they gotta push theirselves into our way of living."

"Hmm."

"Yup. Says if he had his way — the ones that farm here — he'd slaughter 'em like he does his hawgs."

Her eyebrows shot up. "That so? Anything else?"

"Ain't that enough?"

"Sure is. Appreciate the information." She stood and shook his hand. "You can go out the back way if you'd like." She pointed him in the right direction.

"Come on," she motioned to Chucky. They headed west out of Finchville, exceeding the speed limit toward O'Connor's farm. They crossed the overpass of I-80 and turned off the highway onto a two-lane paved road. A few miles in, the pavement changed to gravel. She was forced to slow down to save the undercarriage from the flying rocks. Then the gravel petered out to only dirt.

"Hold up. You passed the driveway."

She hit the brakes and reversed fast. A huge dust cloud enveloped the car. She made a hard right into the driveway and braked by the barn. The car rocked back and forth on its axle. A man in a battered hat and overalls stood by the cattle trough. They piled out of the cruiser. "You Robert O'Connor?"

"Yeah." He walked toward them. "You seem to be in a mighty big rush."

He had that same red, weathered look all the farmers had. Even though the new tractors and combines sheltered them, they still spent many hours in the punishing sun. She showed her badge and introduced themselves. "We want to talk to you about Glory Delgado's death."

"Yeah, heard about that." He scratched the back of his neck.

"Someone in town says you don't like Latinos." She watched his face closely.

He looked from Chucky to her. "Way I see it, she's one less of 'em to worry about." Then he seemed to realize he'd said too much. "True, I don't like 'em pushin' their way in, but you can't think I had anything to do with it."

"You do realize she was Caucasian?"

"Far as I can figure, if you marry a Spic — you are a Spic."

She was dumbfounded at the man's bigotry. "Mr. O'Connor, I need you to come into town and give us a statement. Maybe take a polygraph."

"You can't be serious?"

"Dead serious, sir."

As they drove back through town with O'Connor in the back seat, people stopped on the street to stare.

They escorted their newest suspect into her office and started the recorder. O'Connor gave his statement without the slightest embarrassment. It was hard for her to wrap her mind around how someone whose ancestors had once been referred to as "dirty Irishmen," could demonstrate that same prejudice toward another minority.

When they finished the interview, the man said, "I'd like you to take me home now."

"But we have a small problem, Mr. O'Connor — you have no alibi," she said.

"Guess that's true — not unless the cattle start talking." He glared. "S'pose I'll have to take one 'a those tests."

"Okay, follow me." She headed to the equipment room and grabbed a deputy on her way to administer the polygraph. Deidre stepped out and watched through a one-way mirror. No red flags in his body language. No fidgets or nervous tics. And the fact that he was willing to take a polygraph was usually another sign of innocence. *Dammit. Even if he passes, I'm keeping an eye on this guy. And I wonder how many more like him we've got running around out there?*

Chapter 14

"**K**en'ra, Ken'ra!" Toni tugged at her pants leg.
"What?" The refreshment line at the movie was at a standstill.

"Toni wants candy," her sister whined.

"Toni? Who's Toni?" she teased.

Large tears pooled in the little girl's eyes.

"Oh, that's right. I know you." She patted Toni's head. "You're my little sis. Sorry sweetie, but Mom gave us just enough money for a popcorn to share."

The toddler turned her tear-filled gaze to Johnny who stood with his arm looped around Kendra. "Please?" she pleaded.

Johnny pulled his jeans pockets out. "Sorry. Empty."

Ignoring her sister's pouty expression, she said, "Geez, I hope we get to the front of this line before the movie starts."

"Hey Kenny, just had an idea. You know how you've been stessin' about Audrey being jealous of me?"

"Yeah."

"Well, there's this new kid who just moved from Columbus. He's on my soccer team. Seems pretty cool."

"And?"

"Why don't we do a double date?"

She thought about it all of two seconds. "Okay, if you think Audrey will like him."

He released his hold on her to do a little victory shuffle. "Great. I'll ask Lucas if Friday works. But do you think she'll go for it?"

"Leave her to me," she said.

"Hey, gonna hit the Men's."

"No problem. Probably still be here when you get back." As the line inched along, she looked around at the other moviegoers. She was surprised to see Alex in the line opposite her.

"Hi," she said.

"Hey." He sounded a little friendlier this time.

"Who you here with?"

"Nobody."

She couldn't imagine going to a movie alone. "Hey, sit with us. Johnny's here, too."

"Nah. That's okay."

"C'mon, I'm sure Johnny's feeling outnumbered." She glanced down at Toni and rolled her eyes.

"Dunno. Maybe."

When Johnny returned, she pointed out Alex, whose line was moving so fast he was nearly at the counter. "He's here alone. I asked him to sit with us."

He raised an eyebrow. "Remember what you promised?"

"Absolutely. This has zero to do with the case. He needs a friend."

"He's a dork," Johnny argued.

"Since when did you sign up for snob mode?" For the first time, she felt a flash of anger toward him.

"You promise you're givin' up the Sherlock Holmes thing?"

"Johnny!" she said in exasperation.

Toni, who had been listening to every word, echoed Kendra, "Johnny!"

"All right." He raised his hands in surrender. "I'll go get him and meet you inside."

By the time the girls got their popcorn, the theater was dark and the previews flickered on the screen. Eventually, Kendra saw the boys waving at them in the darkness and pulled Toni along with her free hand.

"Wanna sit by Johnny," Toni whined.

Kendra reluctantly stationed her sister between Johnny and herself. *So much for making out. Just as well. Toni would tell on me anyway.* Alex was sitting on the other side of Johnny. *No chance to talk to him now. Shoot.*

As the film's ending credits rolled, they headed to the lobby. "Did you like the movie?" she asked Alex.

"It was okay."

"We're headed over to Audrey's. Wanna come?"

Johnny gave her a dark look.

"Gotta get home to Dad," Alex said. "My ride's probably out front."

Kendra looked at her watch. "It's too late to help in the fields. He'd even be done with the milking."

"No, I mean he needs me around. It's like he's paralyzed or somethin'. Mostly just sits in Mom's rocker on the porch at night. Doesn't watch TV or nothin'."

"That's gotta be rough," Johnny said.

Kendra saw that it was beginning to dawn on her boy-friend that things weren't so good for Alex.

"I'm used to it. Mom needed me, too. Only in a different way."

"How's that?" she asked.

"Tried to help her with whatever she was doing. Took her a long time — she got distracted easy." He had a far-away look. "Like throwing food containers in the recycle. She'd have to wash every bit of gunk out of them first. Rinse them. Then drain and dry them. It could take hours. If I helped, we got done faster."

"Huh." Johnny stared at Alex in disbelief.

He bobbed his head. "Yeah, she liked it when I helped out. If she was happy, I was, too."

Kendra tried to imagine how hard it must've been to do all that crazy stuff.

"Anyway, Dad says when we're done with the planting, Uncle Manny's going to help us clean up the house. At least we got the kitchen straightened up."

"That's good." She tried to sound encouraging.

"Yeah. How come you're being nice to me?" he asked abruptly.

She shrugged. "Family troubles are the pits. I've had my share." She knew better than to say how sorry she felt for him. *Pride can be a bitch.*

Chapter 15

He wiped the steam from the bathroom mirror and stared into it. "You're not a bad person," he said aloud. "It was an accident." The moisture distorted his image. Inside he felt distorted, too. Everything was out of kilter.

Dropping the towel from his waist, he walked to the bedroom to dress, telling himself to forget about her. But as he pulled a shirt and pants from the closet, he remembered what the ungrateful slut had done to him. He replayed the scene in his head — driving to the farm on a beautiful spring day — hope building that finally his life would change for the better. But she'd treated him like cock roach. A rage began to gather in the pit of his stomach. Blood coursed through his body, hot and fiery. He clenched his fists. He had to hit something.

The sound of splintering wood and a sharp pain in his hand brought him up short. He stared at the closet door and his bloodied knuckles. He wasn't sure how many times he'd struck out, only that the anger now gave way to a black abyss. *All my life I haven't been good enough for women. Why? I'm smart — Christ, I've got a 143 I.Q. so I can carry on an intelligent conversation, unlike a lotta guys around here. I keep myself cleaned up — dress okay — don't even smoke.*

He grabbed the towel from the floor and wrapped it around his bleeding hand, then slumped on the edge of the bed. *I would've done anything for you. Anything you asked. But you claimed you didn't like it when you discovered it was me leaving those little notes under the windshield of your car. Acted like you were upset with me. How was that possible when I could see in your eyes how much you wanted me?*

You were a real bitch. I tried to tell you we'd be so happy that you wouldn't even want to hoard anymore. Could start a new life away from this hellish town. But you didn't get it — said you loved your husband and son. Would never leave them.

Then you shoved me away! I only wanted to feel your skin next to mine, your luscious lips on my mouth, your sexy hips beneath mine. How could you, Glory? How could you? When I loved you more than anything in this world?

He curled into a fetal position, unaware of the tears flowing onto the rumpled sheets.

Chapter 16

"**H**ey, Mom? Can Alex come over for movie night?" Kendra called from her bedroom.

"Alex? Is that a new friend of yours?"

"Yeah." She hoped Mom wouldn't ask his last name. She didn't need anyone else ragging on her about snooping around.

"Don't see why not."

Alex wasn't the only thing new to her life. Having friends over was new, too. It used to be that her mom was so stressed that she didn't dare to ask. Plus, their run-down apartment was a major embarrassment. Worse yet, she never knew when Dad might show up on one of his drunken binges. But over time, she'd learned that Audrey and Johnny liked her for herself — not for what she had — or what her parents were like. What a relief that had been.

"I'm glad you didn't say no, 'cuz I already asked him." She walked into the kitchen.

Teresa smiled and rummaged in her purse for money. "Gutsy little girl, aren't you? Get something good at the Red Box. No violence or bad language. And a kids' one for your little sister."

She knew the drill. Like always, she agreed, and hurried out the door so she'd be back before Alex arrived. At the movie kiosk, she chose three films: a Disney for Toni, a comedy for Mom, and an action one she thought Alex might like. She piled the movies into her backpack and jumped on her bike. As she neared her apartment building, she saw Alex coming toward her from the opposite direction on a skateboard. As he performed jumps and other tricks, arms outstretched for balance, he looked like any other kid — without a care in the world. "Hi! Good timing. Just picked up the flicks. Do you like Johnny Depp?"

"Sure. He's cool."

"Come on. You can meet my mom." She led the way.

At first, he seemed nervous, so she hurried to get the movie started. Even though it was the one she'd chosen for Toni, he didn't seem to mind. "Mom will be in in a minute." As if on cue, Teresa stuck her head around the corner from the kitchen and greeted him. He said hello and turned back to Disney's *Snow White*.

They settled in, munching on peanuts and drinking sodas. It wasn't long before he seemed to relax and sprawled in his chair.

Toni sat on the floor next to him. She watched as her sister kept inching closer to Alex until she had her arm wrapped around his lower leg. It was obvious by his occasional grin whenever Toni asked him a question about the movie that he was enjoying her attention. When the movies ended, Teresa called out to them for a game of Yahtzee. He got down on the floor and crawled around with Toni on his back, whinnying like a horse, and carried her to her chair in the kitchen.

The little girl was delighted.

"Hey, what time is it?" he asked.

"Almost nine," Kendra replied.

"Oh, burn." he said. "Better call my uncle to pick me up. Spending the night there. When I told Dad that you'd invited me over, he said I should get out and have some fun. I hope that means he's doin' a little better." After he made the call, he grabbed his skateboard and headed for the door. "Thanks, Mrs. Morgan. It was a blast. I'll have to catch the Yahtzee next time," he said, his initial shyness gone.

"You're welcome. Come on over any time," Teresa said. She arched her eyebrows at Kendra and she knew she'd have to explain the remark about Alex's dad. The cat would be out of the bag. She hoped she could convince her mom that she only wanted to reach out to a kid who was going through some tough stuff. Unfortunately, Mom knew about her obsession with murder investigations, so it might be a hard sell.

"I'll walk out with you." Kendra grabbed her jacket.

"I wanna go, too!" Toni cried.

"No, you need to brush your teeth, climb into your jammies, and jump in bed. You're already up past your bedtime," Teresa said.

"But I wanna play Ya'zee!" Her lips went out in a pout.

Alex squatted down in front of her. "Thanks for sharing your movie with me. Next time we'll play Yahtzee, okay?"

While they waited together by the bank of mail boxes at the edge of the parking lot, she said, "Toni sure likes you."

"Yeah, I noticed. She's a sweet kid." He cleared his throat. "I had a little sis once."

"Really?" *So that's who the girl in the photo is.*

He looked at her in the dim light of the street lamp and told her about the terrible day his sister had chased their dog into the road and been run over.

She peered at him in the shadows and thought his young face looked old. "Oh, I'm so sorry," she said. "You must miss her like crazy."

"Sure do. Been awful without her. Living with my folks afterwards was like living with a pair of ghosts. And now — now Dad is worse than ever." He shook his head.

"At least I've still got my dog, Riley. At first, Dad was so mad at him, he got his rifle — said he was gonna shoot him."

"Oh no!"

"I was so scared I was shaking all over. When he pointed the gun at Riley, I threw my body over him and said he'd have to kill me first. Then Mom came and pulled the gun away from him."

"I'm so sorry, Alex."

"'S okay. Feels kinda good to unload. Haven't talked to anybody about it, except the shrinks. And they don't count."

"They didn't help?"

"Nah. Just kept tellin' me I shouldn't blame myself — accidents happen — blah, blah, blah. F — n' shrinks."

"But Alex — they're right — it wasn't your fault."

His normally soft voice was suddenly very loud. "'Course it was my fault! I was s'posed to be watchin' her. Sometimes I wish Dad would've shot me that night."

Before she could respond, headlights swung into the parking lot and a car braked in front of them. Without another word, he climbed into his uncle's SUV, leaving her staring into the darkness.

Chapter 17

I do my best thinking when I take a walk, Deidre thought. *So, why do I have permanent brain freeze?* She'd told herself she could accomplish two things at once if she got some exercise before work — discover something she'd overlooked in the investigation and begin to lower the readout on her bathroom scale. As she ambled along the tree-lined avenue, she reviewed the last couple of days in her head. Ricky Delgado's financials had turned up a ton of debt. She knew there was always a lot of investment getting a farm up and running. Even though he'd arrived with all the equipment he needed, the place had been pretty run down. He'd borrowed heavily to replace an old equipment shed that was falling to pieces and to make other smaller, but numerous, repairs.

Besides the note to the bank for the farm improvements, their charge card statements showed numerous purchases every month to Finchville stores. The credit lines were maxed out and the family was only making minimum payments on each one. *Mrs. Delgado was ruining her family's credit with her sickness. Maybe someone she owed money to, had finally had enough.* Deidre knew she was stretching it with that theory. No, bigotry, was a much more likely motive.

Even though O'Connor had passed his polygraph, she hadn't dismissed the idea that he could be the killer. Those tests could be misleading. Also, a few more leads had come in after her visit to Sadie's Café. One man she'd learned about was even more extreme than O'Connor in his hatred of Mexicans.

"They got no right to be here!" Old Zach Mortensen had exclaimed when she'd interviewed him. "We settled this prairie in the 1800's and now they wanna come in here and use our land. I don't think so. And I heard the house is a pigsty. Filthy! Filthy! That's what the house is, and they are, too!" He'd curled his lip in disgust.

She wondered if he knew from personal experience how the inside of the house looked. She'd added him to her list of possible suspects. *What if this was a hate crime and there was more than one killer? Maybe he and O'Connor were in on it together.*

Her thoughts were interrupted by the sound of her cell phone.

"Chief, you better get down here fast." Bianca sounded breathless.

"Good morning to you, too."

"Sorry, but we just got a call from one of Robert O'Connor's neighbors. He found him dead in his barn!"

For a minute, her heart forgot to beat. When she recovered from the shock, she said, "No reason for me to come to the office. I'm not far from home. I'll change and go straight out there. Tell Chucky to meet me. Oh, and call the crime-scene unit and tell them to get to O'Connor's ASAP."

"This is getting to be a habit," Bianca said.

"Yeah, I know, and not a good one." She didn't remember fast-walking back to her house, throwing on her uniform, getting in her car, or reaching the town's edge, but she suddenly focused and turned on the light bar. Ignoring the speedometer, she cursed the grid of country roads. Finally, she turned onto the dirt road that led to O'Connor's farm. In a swirl of dust, the car bounced over the ruts so violently that she felt like she was in a cement mixer. His mailbox loomed into view and she turned sharply into the driveway. No sign of Chucky yet. A man stood by the barn. He pulled off his baseball cap and walked toward her.

She was barely out from behind the steering wheel before he started talking. "His cattle busted through the pasture fence and were milling around in the road. Came over to tell him and there he was." He gestured toward the barn.

"And you are?"

"Sorry. Bit shook up, I guess — Asmussen — Walt Asmussen — I live over there." He pointed toward his farm.

"I'm Chief Goodwin." She reached out and shook his hand. It trembled in her grip.

"I know. Seen you around town when I'm gettin' supplies and such."

"Okay, Mr. Asmussen. How long have you been here?" She grabbed for her notepad.

"Not long. I called you guys as soon as I found him. You sure got here fast."

"Did you touch anything in the barn?"

"Don't think so. I went in and saw him like that and backed out. Couldn't seem to take my eyes off him. I might've steadied myself on the barn door. Not sure."

"All right. Let's go take a look. We'll just stand in the doorway. You might see something that jogs your memory about what you did."

"Have to?"

She stared at the man's pale face. She didn't need him getting sick. "Guess not, but wait here. I may have some questions." She left him sitting on an overturned bucket and tromped up a small incline to the red barn. One thing about barns: they had lots of crossbeams. O'Connor's corpse hung from one of them. An overturned chair lay on its side beneath his body. The flies that usually had a heyday on manure had found a new treat. *Looks like suicide, but the CSU will tell us for sure. Just wish they didn't take forever.*

Maybe he did murder Glory, was stricken with a guilty conscience, and decided to meet his Maker. She wasn't a religious person, but she couldn't help asking herself if there was a God, would He forgive a man whose hate drove him to commit murder?

Her thoughts returned to the scene before her. Somehow, suicide didn't fit O'Connor. He'd been unapologetic about his prejudice. She was pretty sure that if he'd killed Glory, it wouldn't bother him enough to do this.

Things are getting worse by the minute. Times like this I wish I had some friends here I could confide in. I'll call Joanne in Omaha tonight. She heard a car coming in from the road. *Probably Chucky.*

She walked back out to their witness. "Mr. Asmussen, before you head back to your place, do you know if he had any family in the area?"

"Uh, ex-wife and daughter live over in Fremont. Dorothy left him a long time ago. Don't think they stay in touch much."

"Okay, we'll look for some contacts in the house. Do you think you could help with the livestock? Hard telling how long since the cattle were milked. Probably why they busted down the fence."

"I'm sure of it. I'll round 'em up and take 'em to my place for now. He's only got a dozen or so, and they're tagged. I'll feed the goats and chickens real quick, too."

"Much appreciated. But stay away from the barn." She shook his hand.

"No need to be tellin' me that," he said, as he hurried away to his farm for chicken feed.

She turned to Chucky. "Well, let's go. Body's in the barn."

Chapter 18

The day Kendra had been looking forward to with mixed emotions had finally arrived: the big double date. She hadn't admitted to Johnny that she'd never skated in her life. Apparently, this was what Lucas had suggested and she didn't want to mess up a chance for Audrey to find a boyfriend. *How hard can rolling around on 8 wheels be, right? I'm sure I can pull it off.* It'd sure be fun to do stuff together — the four of them. What made it extra cool was that Johnny's friend was sixteen and had his driver's license. In fact, he was picking them up this afternoon at Mickey D's to drive to the Skate Deck in Grand Island.

"Do you know what kind of car he has?" she asked Johnny while they waited on the sidewalk.

"I think he drives his dad's second car — a Honda Camry or something."

Her BFF was being unusually quiet. Kendra figured she was either caught up in the excitement of meeting Lucas, or feeling guilty about deceiving her parents. They were super-protective — especially her dad. That was one reason they'd decided to go during the day while Mr. Worth was at work. She remembered back to what they'd had to go through just to start up their little lawn service. It'd been a real pain. He'd acted like they were launching a huge start up — micro managing the contract he insisted they have — making sure they outlined how their profits would be divided — whose lawn equipment they'd use — yada, yada, yada.

But Audrey's mom was less vigilant, so it'd been easy to get permission to meet with her and Johnny. Mrs. Worth had met Johnny before, and of course, she knew Kendra well. Audrey had said nothing at all about Lucas. If Mr. Worth had been there, he would've quizzed his daughter until she revealed all the details of the meetup.

"I feel so bad lying to Mom," Audrey said.

"You didn't really lie to her. Just didn't tell her everything."

"Come on. You know better." She'd set her pretty lips into a thin line and glared.

"I know. But you're not a little kid anymore. And that's the way they treat you."

Audrey fell silent.

Her own mom always worked long hours, so if she wanted to do something, all she had to do was leave a note about what she was doing and when she'd be home and her mom was happy. There'd been many times when she'd fudged what she was up to, and her mom hadn't been any wiser. She wasn't sure what Johnny had told his mom about today, but from what she could tell, parents were more lenient with sons than daughters when it came to dating. *Maybe because boys can't get pregnant.* A silver car pulled up in front of them, interrupting her thoughts.

The tinted passenger window went down and a redheaded boy called, "Hop in."

Johnny got in the front seat while she went around the car and got in the back seat behind Lucas. Audrey took the back seat, passenger side. After they were buckled in, her friend leaned over and whispered in her ear, "Do I look okay?"

"Fantastic," she whispered back.

"This is Kendra and Audrey," Johnny said, waving toward the back seat.

"Hey," Lucas said, and pulled away from the curb.

"Hi. Nice ride," Kendra said. *That sounded lame.*

"Thanks. Dad lets me drive it sometimes."

She glanced over at Audrey and saw she was checking Lucas out. Her friend turned to her and grinned. *So far, so good.*

The ride to Grand Island was short and they were in plenty of time for the afternoon skate. They piled out of the Honda and skirted the potholes in the parking lot to the ticket booth. Johnny paid for Kendra's ticket, but Audrey and Lucas bought their own.

As they walked in, the sound of organ music met them and she could see through the windows of the inner doors that a mirror ball hung from the ceiling, throwing patterns on the walls and floor.

"Lucas and I'll go get the skates. Meet us over there." Johnny pointed to some benches.

"Might be nice if we knew their sizes, dude," Lucas said. They all laughed.

"Well, whadja think?" Kendra asked, as soon as the boys were out of earshot.

"He's very cute," Audrey said. "Seems nice, too."

"Yeah, I think he's cool," she agreed. Inside, she was doing the happy dance.

It wasn't long before the boys were back and Johnny dropped a pair of roller skates at her feet. Suddenly, her stomach was queasy. *Wonder how many other people have worn these?* They were so old that the boot tops flopped to the side, and one lace had busted and been knotted back together. Her nose was assaulted with the smell of dirty feet, stale popcorn and oiled wood. She glanced at her friends who seemed oblivious to her anxiety and were busily lacing up their skates. Finally, she took a gulp of air and forced her feet into the horrible things.

Johnny grabbed up all their shoes and said he'd be back as soon as he found a locker.

She watched him skate smoothly back to her. *Now the truth comes out.* "Um, Johnny?"

"Yeah?"

"I've never done this before."

"What? I wondered why you were stalling." He laughed.

"Yeah, guess I'm a little nervous. And the smell of these things makes me feel like I'm gonna hurl."

"Better not to think about who all's worn 'em." He bent and began tying one skate for her while her shaky fingers worked on the other.

"Well, come on. Skating's a snap. You'll love it." He held his hand out to her and they all made their way to the rink.

He's right — this is fun, she thought, as she glided across the carpet. But the second she stepped onto the wood floor, her skates went out from under her, she lost her grip on Johnny's hand, and she went down — hard.

He was helping her up before she knew what'd happened. "You okay?"

She was fine, except for being so humiliated she wanted to cry. She looked at her friends' faces and could see they were trying very hard not to laugh.

"Lucas, you get on one side of her and I'll take the other," Johnny directed. And so, it went. She found herself wishing they could hold her vertical all afternoon. They took her around and around until she began to get used to the feel of the skates and floor beneath her.

"You're doing so-o-o-o good," Audrey said in her most encouraging voice as she flew by.

Eventually, she tried it without her escorts, and crashed down again. They helped her up. She shook them off and perilously skated a few feet to the outer wall of the rink. She used that for balance as she slowly maneuvered around the rink by herself. She noticed she wasn't the only one falling down. That helped. And she loved the piped-in organ music. The announcer called out different instructions, like "Ladies' choice" and "Reverse direction."

And even better, Audrey and Lucas skated arm in arm. "Looks like our plan worked," she said to Johnny when he swooped in behind her. "But what were the chances of them both having red hair?" She laughed.

He grinned in return. "Look around you, Kenny. Haven't you noticed how many fair-skinned blondes and redheads there are?"

She thought about that. *True, there are a lot of Scandinavians here. Including me. Mom says I'm mostly Swedish. My ancestors from way back were pioneers.* Then a disturbing thought hit her. *What if I get trapped here like them, where there's nothing to do but farm or run a small business in town? Not gonna happen. I'm gettin' out of here soon as I'm old enough.*

"You're right, Johnny. But can you imagine what their kids would look like? Major carrot tops."

"Don't get ahead of yourself, girl." He wagged his finger at her and smiled. "They're just fixin' to start high school and this is their first date."

The session flew by, and the man behind the microphone thanked them for turning out, and invited them back again, "real soon." People were flocking to return their skates, except for the ones who had hopes of becoming professionals. Johnny told her they were staying for lessons.

"Hey, after we turn in our skates, why don't we hang out and watch the ones who really know how it's done?" Lucas asked.

Kendra looked at her friend. *Would she be worried about getting back?*

"Dad won't be home for a couple hours. Let's do it," Audrey said.

There was a crowd who had the same idea as their little group, and they settled themselves in the middle of them.

They all oohed and aahed at the difficult dance steps and jumps performed by the costumed skaters.

"How can they do that?" Kendra marveled aloud.

"Must've been born with skates on their feet," Lucas said.

As they watched, she overheard a man and a woman talking next to her.

"Did you hear the latest?" the man asked.

"What?" the woman replied.

"They found another dead body, over Finchville way."

"Where'd you hear that?"

"On the noon news today," he said.

It took every ounce of restraint Kendra could muster not to turn and look at the pair. She stared fixedly ahead.

"Who was it?" the woman asked.

"Some farmer. Announcer said it was an apparent suicide."

At last, she couldn't contain herself. She elbowed Johnny. "Did you hear that?" she muttered.

"What?" he asked.

"The people next to me said Finchville's got another dead body. Possible suicide," she whispered.

"What?" Johnny turned to her and Kendra repeated what she'd overheard.

"So?" he asked.

His tone of voice left little doubt about what he was thinking. She looked away.

"You want to get involved again, don't you? Man, what is it with you and dead people?"

She shrugged.

"It's a suicide, for Christ's sake!" Johnny exclaimed.

People turned to stare.

"What's going on?" Lucas asked.

Johnny jumped up, grabbing her by the arm. "Nothing. Let's go."

She yanked her arm away, but followed him out of the building with Audrey and Lucas close behind. Sure, maybe she was a screw up, but that didn't mean Johnny could touch her that way. After what Mom had been through with Dad, there was no way she'd let a guy manhandle her.

The ride back was a downer. Lucas and Audrey tried to make conversation, but Johnny sat with his arms folded across his chest, and didn't utter a word.

So much for a good time, she thought.

Chapter 19

"Joanne?" Deidre responded to her best friend's hello. "You don't sound so good. Everything okay? Haven't heard from you in ages. Would've called, but figured you were gettin' comfortable with the new job."

"I wish. I've fallen into a new case with two murder vics. It's got me on the edge of a nervous breakdown."

"I'm putting you on speaker a sec. This sounds like a one-glass-of-wine call — maybe two," Joanne said.

She could hear the clink of a glass and the sound of liquid gurgling. "Man, oh man, you got that right. It was bad enough when an innocent farm wife turned up dead. The only concrete thing we've got is an unknown DNA close to her body. And today a man was found hanged in his barn." she blurted.

"You're not serious." Joanne said.

"If only. The medical people are calling the second one a suicide for now. But no lab results back yet."

"But you're thinking it wasn't?"

"The guy didn't strike me as the type. Plus, we found a possible link between him and the murdered woman."

Her friend had worked in the same precinct with her in Omaha before she'd landed the job in Finchville. While they'd worked together, they'd struck a close bond. Joanne was still pounding the streets of Nebraska's largest city. She didn't miss that a bit — her feet would hurt like crazy at the end of the day — but she did miss hanging out with her friend. Now they talked on the phone often, and tried to meet up at least once a month. She regretted that she hadn't called sooner, but the mayhem in her town had taken over her life.

"What link?" Joanne asked.

"The murdered woman — Glory Delgado — her husband is Latino, and the old guy they found hanged — he hated anybody who wasn't as white as sliced bread. He'd even made threats."

"Anything specific against the family?"

"Not that I know of." She rubbed her forehead. "But when I interviewed him, he sure didn't hang back about how much he hated Mexicans."

"Hmm. What else you got?"

"On the first case — the woman — the family owed a lot of money. And she was a hoarder — bought stuff all over town. Should've seen their house — someone lit a match, they'd never get out alive. Anyway, I'm wondering if one of the store owners carrying their debt got fed up and killed her."

"Seems far-fetched to me," Joanne said.

"Yeah, me too. But honestly, so does the racist angle."

"I'm sure you checked to see if she was having an affair? Husband's not good for it?"

"'Course. Hubby does have a bad temper — a couple of domestics since they moved here — even an old record for assault against a guy — but my gut tells me it's not him."

"Your gut was always right on when we worked together. Anything else? Boyfriend, maybe?"

"Not that we've found, but the vic did have a soft spot for the down-and-out. She'd give 'em handouts — even clothes. Turns out that some of her buys were for men's clothing, but not in her husband's size."

"That angle sounds like it might pan out," Joanne said. "Maybe one of the homeless guys wanted a little more than freebies, and it went bad."

"Yeah, I questioned a couple of 'em, but ended up clearing them both. We get so many of those guys, with the railroad running through here. There could've easily been one that I don't know about. But there's one thing that makes me think it wasn't a homeless dude."

"Yeah?"

"There was the definite aroma of a man's cologne lingering over her body at the crime-scene. Guys riding the rails don't ever smell *that* good. And I checked — the husband doesn't wear cologne." She sighed.

"You're right — sounds unlikely it's a vagrant — but if it is, it'll be a tough case to crack. They're hard to find since most of 'em live off the grid."

"Tell me something I don't know. But, hey, thanks for listening. I needed to vent."

"I see why you're stressed out. Maybe you'll catch a break when Omaha gets the results back on the latest death. Hang in there And, keep me in the loop, okay?"

They chatted a little while longer. Joanne told her how she was jockeying for a promotion in her department. Deidre tried to sound excited for her friend, but knew she wasn't pulling it off. When they said their goodbyes, she stared sullenly at the phone a few minutes. She thought she'd feel better after their talk, but she didn't.

Chapter 20

"**K**endra, up and at 'em," Teresa called. She fought her way through a disturbing web of dreams to wakefulness. "Yeah, Mom," she slurred. She rubbed her eyes and sat on the edge of her bed seeking consciousness and relief from the old nightmares.

The edge of the photo of the Delgado family peeked at her from beneath her pillow. Every day she took the picture with her to school and placed it back under her pillow at night. *Is that weird? Since I'm embarrassed to tell anyone I'm doing it, yeah, it probably is.*

She gazed at the photo for the thousandth time. The little girl leaned out from Glory's arms to whoever was taking the picture. She was laughing. Kendra thought maybe the girl, whom she now knew as Sophie, wanted to play. The family's skin shone in the sun. Their eyes sparkled. They were dressed casually, in bright colors. *Proud parents. Happy kids. Probably a day with family and friends.*

She stuck the picture in the pocket of her backpack and headed for the shower.

"Hey," Teresa called. "Could you do me a favor on your way to school?"

"What?" She detoured into her mom's room.

"I found this really cute dress at the thrift store, but it's got a stain, right here." Teresa was standing in front of her mirror and holding a lavender dress against her body. She pointed at a dark spot by the waistline. "Drop it at the cleaners on your way to school. Be sure to have them write down where this spot is on the receipt," she instructed. "It's all rayon, so I can't wash it. Don't let 'em charge you more than four bucks."

She took the dress and jammed it into a plastic shopping bag and shoved it hard into the top of her backpack. She felt something like a rock settling in her stomach. Her mom had started dating again. *I know she needs a social life, but she'll probably get taken in by another loser.*

From the hallway, she saw her little sister crunching on her Rice Krispies in the kitchen. *Gee, Mom hasn't dated anyone since way before Toni was born. That's like over five years. Guess I should tweak my attitude.* "Hurry up. We gotta leave early so I can go by the cleaners," she called to Toni.

"See you this afternoon." She bent to give her sister a peck on the cheek.

"Okay, Ken'ra." Toni grabbed her Barbie from her backpack and raced into the playroom of the daycare.

She smiled at the sight and headed for the cleaners, just a block away. She pushed through the door. The woman behind the counter seemed rushed, and frowned when Kendra requested the stain be noted on the receipt. But she insisted.

"A little pushy for a kid," the woman said.

"No. Just doing what my mom asked," she replied. "And it won't be more than four dollars, right?" She smiled at the woman. As the main errand runner for the family, she'd dealt with enough people like this to know how to stand her ground.

The woman handed her the receipt. "Have a nice day," she said icily.

She nodded and hurried away to meet up with Audrey. She hoped her friend hadn't been waiting long at their usual spot. "Hi. Sorry I'm late."

"No prob. I had so much fun at the skate deck." Audrey said.

"Whadja think of Lucas?" She knew the answer, but wanted to hear more.

"He's so cool."

They giggled.

"But — you and Johnny. Not so good?" Audrey asked, giving her friend a look.

"Guess not," she said glumly.

"You need to stop nosing around. You did it with Cloud, and now with this Glory woman. And you're even imagining there's some connection with that old geezer that hung himself. You can't be doing this crap. You'll lose Johnny. And besides that, it's crazy dangerous."

"I know. But I think about that Delgado kid, and how sad he is, and I wanna help him."

"Do you think finding his mom's killer will help? You're smarter than that. It won't bring her back."

She knew Audrey was right. *How do I get rid of this voice in my head telling me to do this stuff?* "Are you going to the soccer game Friday night?" she asked, hoping to get her friend off her rant. But she was far from done.

"I'm serious, Kendra. You're stupid and arrogant. You need to stop — now!"

"Arrogant? No way."

"Yeah, you are. You think the rules don't apply to you and you can do whatever the hell you want. And that's not all. You manipulate people to fit into your little schemes. I don't like it, and Johnny doesn't either."

She stared at her friend. She knew Audrey and Johnny were fed up with her playing detective, but she was shocked to hear that they thought she was using them.

Audrey pulled her iPod from her pocket and roughly inserted her ear buds. End of conversation.

Kendra's eyes stung with tears as they walked silently the rest of the way to class.

Chapter 21

Deidre's ear felt sweaty from holding the phone so closely. "You've finished O'Connor's autopsy and you're classifying the cause of death as "Strangulation," but conditions contributing to death listed as 'Undetermined" — not Homicide — or Suicide?"

The Omaha Medical Examiner, Kenneth Tate, had explained his findings more than a few times — this was the sort of ambiguity that drove her nuts. She'd seen it before. Medical examiners didn't want to go out on a limb. They believed homicide units were the ones responsible for proving cause of death.

It was so rare to have a possible murder in these parts that Tate had made a special trip to Grand Island to perform the autopsy. Normally, if an autopsy were deemed necessary — for instance if someone young died — a local funeral home performed the procedure at the request of one of Grand Island's county attorneys.

The man continued, "That's right. I've got my doubts about cause of death, so I'm asking for an inquest. The judge can take it from there."

"What makes you think it's not suicide?" She perked up.

"One thing. The ligature marks and internal examination of the neck and spine appeared consistent with suicide, but the torso had some lacerations I can't explain."

Lacerations? What lacerations? "Can I drive over and take a look at the body this morning? I'd like to see those cuts you're talking about."

"Sure," he said. "The body is at Franklin Funeral Home on Faidley Avenue. I won't be there, but I'll tell the mortician to expect you." He said something about finishing up the paperwork and the line went dead.

Deidre tried to keep the excitement she felt at this new development from her voice as she called to Chucky, "Wanna take a ride over to Grand Island?"

He appeared instantly at the door of her office. "What's up?"

She gathered her cell phone and keys. "O'Connor. Got some mysterious marks on his body."

He turned very pale. "Never looked at a body in a drawer before. Do I have to?"

"Up to you. If you wanna move up in the department, it's something you're gonna have to get used to."

She watched him mentally grapple with the decision. He was probably thinking about his young wife, Alicia. She was counting on him to make a good living so she could stay home with the kids.

Finally, he said, "Lead the way, chief. But I'm mystified about what marks the M.E.'s talkin' about. There wasn't any blood on O'Connor that I saw."

"Roger that," she agreed. "But, if the stains were small, maybe we missed them. Remember he wore that plaid shirt in rusts and browns?"

In the cruiser, she fought the urge to turn on the light bar so she could speed. *Better set the right example for Chucky this time.* She leaned back in the seat and tried to let the fragrant smell of alfalfa blooming beside the road calm her nerves.

A short time later, they navigated Grand Island's many stop lights and arrived at their destination. Pulling into the parking lot of the funeral home, she parked beside a black hearse. She gave her passenger a sideways glance. His fists were clenched. "Listen, it'll help if you don't look at his face. What I need is for you to check out the lacerations on the torso. That's all you have to do, okay?"

He nodded, and they entered into a large room with doors leading off in several directions. Beside one door, a candle burned on a table with what appeared to be a guest book. *That must be where they hold the viewings.* Where the other doors led remained a mystery. She loudly cleared her throat.

"I'll be right there," a voice called from somewhere. Seconds later, one of the doors opened to reveal a graying man in a tailored suit. "You must be from Finchville," he said when he saw their uniforms. He came forward to shake their hands and introduced himself as the funeral director.

She thought he had just the right firmness in his hand-shake for someone in the business of soothing grief stricken loved ones — solid, but not overly so.

"Mr. Tate said you'd be along." Wasting no time, he turned and led them through one of the doors, down a short hallway and into a large room. This was where bodies were prepared for burial, and if necessary, autopsies performed. High windows gave lots of light, yet afforded privacy. Everything was stainless steel from the sinks to the examination tables to the bank of drawers. The man knew exactly where Mr. O'Connor was resting. He went directly to one of the drawers and extended it.

He removed the sheet to a few inches below O'Connor's waist and stepped back. Deidre went to stand on one side of the body while Chucky walked to the opposite side. True to what Kenneth Tate had told her, there were tiny lacerations in the man's side. They were on the side closest to Chucky, but she could still see a couple of them. "Hmm. What do you think?" She looked up at him and saw only the top of his head. "Chucky?" Suddenly, he began to weave from side to side. She hurried around the drawer and guided him to a nearby chair.

"Sorry." He bent to put his head between his legs.

"Take deep breaths." She walked back to the body. "Mind if I take a few photos?" she asked the funeral director.

"Not at all. If you're going to be a while, I can leave."

"No, just need a couple of minutes." She took several shots of the ligature marks and puncture wounds. She lowered the sheet to expose his entire body, but could see no other damage. The marks around the neck looked consistent with a hanging death. But the wounds to the torso had her stumped.

They thanked the mortician and walked to the cruiser. She gave her officer a little time to regroup. "You okay now?"

"Yeah — sorry about that. I didn't look at his face, honest," he said. "But I did get a look at the marks before I started goin' all wobbly. So, what do you think they are?"

"Not sure. They were evenly spaced and very small. Looked like it could've been done in one motion. Some sort of tool around the farm, maybe?"

"That's what I was thinking."

Back in the office, Deidre put in a call to the crime-scene unit in Grand Island. "I'm calling about the Robert O'Connor case," she told the head of the unit.

"I was just going to call you," he said.

"Oh?"

"The Omaha lab found an unknown sample of DNA on Robert O'Connor. Ran it through CODIS. Unfortunately, no match."

"Damn."

"But one thing which will interest you."

"What?"

"It's the same unidentified DNA we found at the Delgado crime-scene."

She gasped. "Really?"

"I wouldn't make that up."

My hunch was right! O'Connor wasn't the type to commit suicide. Then she remembered the reason for her call. "Hey, did your guys remove any weapons or tools from O'Connor's barn?"

"No weapons — unless you count the rope. And there was a pitchfork close to the body," he said. "We brought it in to check for DNA because the victim's shirt had minute blood trace."

"My God! That's what the wounds were from!" Deidre exclaimed. "The killer must've used the pitchfork to force O'Connor onto the chair."

"Sounds likely. We didn't find any of the unknown DNA on the 'fork's handle, so the killer probably wore gloves — but you know these guys always mess up somehow. No exception here. We found a few brown hairs on the chair and since O'Connor was bald as a newborn babe, we checked it for DNA. Got lucky — there was a follicle on one strand. Maybe the vic grabbed at him when he was being urged onto the chair. Anyway, bingo. That's how we got the sample."

She heard the satisfaction in his voice, and she wanted to break into a dance herself. Maybe this was the break they needed. "You'll send your written report over right away?"

"Absolutely," he said.

Chapter 22

Kendra grabbed her sandwich and apple from her locker and headed to the lunchroom to meet Audrey, Johnny, and Lucas. As usual, the din was almost earsplitting, with the clatter of cheap silverware and kids shouting to one another across the room. She made her way around the lunch line, which snaked nearly to the door. She looked over to see Alex Delgado in his usual spot.

Audrey had forgiven her for her interest in O'Connor's death, but she hadn't seen Johnny since the trip to the skate deck. Today she was determined to apologize.

"Hey," she said as she scooted in beside him. Audrey and Lucas answered, but he didn't respond. Their legs touched beneath the table, and her pulse raced. "You're right. I'm not a cop and it's none of my business what happened to that farmer." She laid her hand on his arm.

He pulled away, stared straight ahead, and continued shoveling mac-and-cheese in his mouth, then said, "That was some hat trick you pulled off last night, Lucas."

"Really. I was wrong, Johnny." She almost choked on the words. It hurt to admit she'd screwed up, but it pained her more to have him ignore her.

Silence hung in the air. Audrey and Lucas eyed each other. After what seemed like days, Johnny said, "Uh huh."

She took a deep breath. "Audrey knows — told her I'm butting out of all that stuff." She knew she was begging, but suddenly didn't care. All that mattered was his forgiveness.

He drank down a half carton of milk and finally turned to look at her. "Sure 'bout that?"

"Swear on my dead grandma's grave!"

He stared levelly at her. Then a little smile played across his lips. "Okay then." He put his arm around her and pulled her close. She leaned into him with a sigh of relief.

"Oh brother. Look at the lovebirds," Lucas kidded. "Can we please get back to talking about the soccer game and my awesomeness in it?"

But even as they chattered about soccer and their next double date, Kendra's eyes wandered over to Alex's table. *Stop it.* She remembered Audrey calling her arrogant and manipulative. And Johnny's rejection had hurt her to the bone. *I've got to change. Somehow. This is the first time in years I've had good friends. I can't mess it up.*

Chapter 23

"Yes, Your Honor," Deidre replied. "I was the first law enforcement officer to view Robert O'Connor's body."

The judge peered down from his bench at her. "Please tell the court the condition of the deceased and the scene in general." The old courtroom smelled faintly of mold, sweat and a powerful industrial cleaner. At one time, it'd been the crown jewel of Grand Island, but many decades of use had reduced it to creaking wooden floors and cracked marble. The magistrate looked as decrepit as the building, but there was a definite spark in his eyes — his body might be failing him, but his mind was as sharp as the day he was inducted.

As she recounted the crime-scene and her actions there, she thought to herself how much she hated inquest proceedings. But they were a necessary evil, and surely the witnesses and evidence would convince the judge that O'Connor's death needed further investigation.

After her own testimony, she listened to O'Connor's neighbor, Walt Asmussen, tell how he'd discovered the body. Then Chucky gave his account. She thought he did well, considering it was his first time testifying in court. Finally, the head of the crime-scene unit presented the lab's findings.

"All right. I think we've heard from everyone," the judge said. "I'll read over all the evidence and give my decision to you by tomorrow. Oh — Chief Goodwin — one more thing."

Surprised, she looked up. "Yes, Your Honor?"

"Why wasn't the pitchfork in your original written report?"

She felt her face grow red. "I'm sorry, Judge. There was a lot of hay on the floor and we didn't want to contaminate the scene. My deputy and I took a brief look. I guess we missed it."

He frowned at her. "Try to be more thorough next time."

"Yes, Your Honor. Won't happen again, Your Honor." She wanted to crawl under the table.

Outside on the sidewalk, Chucky said, "Hey, don't feel bad. You told me how the CSU always rips us for trashing their crime-scenes."

"I know. We can't win for losing." But she knew the judge was right. She'd screwed up. She should've seen the tears in O'Connor's shirt, too.

And to make matters worse, even though she now had two murders, she had zero leads. *The only link between the victims is the racist angle. Does Finchville have a secret society of hate mongers like the Ku Klux Klan?* The hair on the back of her neck stood up. *If O'Connor was a member, maybe he knew about, or even took part in, Glory's death. Later, he might've been stricken with guilt and threatened to turn himself in, so the group killed him.*

"When we get back to the office, I'm going to keep checking on this racial thing. And I want you to go back through the files on both cases. Then start talking to everyone we interviewed again."

"Everyone?" Chucky pulled a long face.

"Everyone." she said. "And something else — do you remember the man's fragrance we detected around Glory's body?"

"Yeah, it was something different — not the usual Old Spice or Aqua Velva the guys usually wear around here."

"Good. So, keep your nose on the alert when you're interviewing the men."

"But if we do find someone who wears that cologne, it wouldn't fly as evidence."

She gave him a withering glance. "I know that, but at least it'd give us a possible suspect."

It was mid-afternoon — the perfect time to pay Sadie a visit at the café. The dinner rush would be over, and supper customers wouldn't be coming in yet. "Sadie, get me a piece of that delicious homemade cherry pie and some coffee," she said. She slid into a booth furthest from the few customers there.

When Sadie brought her order, she asked her to sit.

"What's up?" Sadie asked, settling into her seat. She sighed. "Sure feels good to give the old bones a rest for a minute."

"Know what you mean — my hips kill me if I do too much walkin'. Hey, when I was in the other day, a couple of fellas told me there were some bad attitudes about Latinos farming the land."

"Yeah, and one of 'em is layin' up in a metal drawer."

"Yup — and I don't want the Grand Island mortuary getting any more of that kind of business from us. I know you hear a lot when you're refilling coffee cups. Who else shared O'Connor's view?"

"Nobody I know of," the woman said. She looked out the window. "Nice day, huh?"

Deidre stared at the woman. "You know Sadie, I'm trained to recognize when I'm being lied to." She took a sip of coffee and waited.

Sadie gulped. "If I rat 'em out and they're that damned crazy, how do I know I won't be next?"

"Normally, I'd be sympathetic to your cause. But right now, I don't care. We've gotta get this thing solved. And trust me, no one will hear where I got my information."

The anxious woman slapped the edge of the table with the towel she had draped over her shoulder. "Oh, all right." She looked down the way to be sure she wasn't being overheard, and said in a low voice, "Bunch of 'em troop in here every Saturday morning after they drop off their eggs and produce at the creamery. They squat in that big booth in the back. 'Course they talk about the price of livestock and how the weather's gonna affect their crops, but they always have time to rag on those poor hard-working people. I just don't get it. They're not hurting nobody."

Deidre pulled her pad and pen from her pocket. "I need names. All of them."

Sadie had come up with four more men's names besides O'Connor and the other fellow she'd already talked to — Zach Mortenson. She'd crossed him off her list when she'd learned he was visiting family in Georgia when Glory had died. It would be hard checking these new men's alibis for O'Connor, since his time of death wasn't clear. They'd been given a 24-hour window by the medical examiner — somewhere between four in the afternoon and four the next morning. The fact that his cattle had busted through the fence led her to believe that they hadn't been milked the evening before — and definitely not in the morning. Most farmers did their milking in the late afternoon, before their supper, so she believed O'Connor had likely died in the late afternoon, or early evening.

Deidre and Chucky immediately set out to talk to the men individually. They all lived within a five-mile radius of O'Connor's farm. The first two men they'd searched out in their fields. Telling them to shut down their tractors, they'd talked to them there in the freshly plowed furrows. Chucky took copious notes while she quizzed them.

When the first farmer had learned why they were there, he'd jumped from his tractor, kicked at the clods of dirt, and muttered obscenities. Once he calmed down, he grudgingly gave his whereabouts on the days of both murders. She and Chucky tromped over the grooved rows to their car with a bad taste in their mouths. The second interview had been more civil, but yielded the same non-results.

They'd caught the other two men at their supper in the early evening, where they were invited to sit with them and their wives at their kitchen tables. The men all had the same weathered faces and calloused, meaty hands of those who made their living off the land. While they made no secret of how they felt about Latinos, they denied knowing anything about the deaths.

To her dismay, their stories all checked out. Examining their activities had consumed more precious time. With each day that passed, she felt more and more frustrated. She was at a dead end. And with the second death, the town of Finchville descended into a sort of panic. Activity languished on the streets, and women and children refused to walk anywhere alone.

Chapter 24

"**N**ice!" Kendra yelled at Johnny. She watched him under the glow of the stadium lights. He flew down the field, effortlessly passing the ball to his teammates. The center forward dribbled closer to the goal, then sent a well-placed chip shot to Johnny, who curved his lithe body into a u-shape and jumped into the air for a header. Goal!

She saw firsthand why her boyfriend liked having Lucas on the team. He was a phenomenal fullback with a kick that spanned the length of the field. She glanced at Audrey sitting beside her and saw by the sappy look on her face that she was smitten with Lucas. So far, Audrey's crush on Lucas had wiped out her BFF's fits of jealousy. She wanted to clinch that, so she'd reassured her friend that she had no long-term plans for Johnny. "There's no way I'd be a farmer's wife — workin' from dawn to dusk — muckin' out horse stalls — collectin' eggs from hens, that don't want to give up their unborn." Deep down, she'd wondered if her words were really true. She was pretty sure they were. Besides all the hard work, she knew she wouldn't like the isolation — just talking to people when she went into town, or visiting with neighbors if they happened to stop by. She was too social for that kind of life.

In spite of the mysterious deaths in their community, most of the town had turned out for the home game. Safety in numbers. And besides, what else was there to do on a Friday night? Come fall there'd be football, which was even more popular. But for now, the only other choices were a movie. Or for the older crowd, drinking at the local bars. Finchville was like all the small towns in Nebraska — there was no shortage of taverns and churches. Drinking and praying were the two main activities, with sports coming in a close third.

A loud whistle from the head referee announced the end of the first period, and she told Audrey she was headed to the Ladies Room. "Wanna come?"

Her friend shook her head as she watched Lucas coming toward her from the backfield to say "hi."

Kendra climbed down from the bleachers and headed toward the concession area. Weaving her way through the crowd, she felt a light tap on her shoulder. When she turned, she was surprised to see Alex.

"Hi," he said.

A pinprick of guilt stabbed at her. She'd been avoiding him so she wouldn't be tempted to get back into the case. She'd even put the photo of his family face-down in her bottom dresser drawer. "How're things?"

"Not bad, I guess." He looked away. "Sometimes I can't sleep though. I get up and Dad's sitting there in the dark. It's creepy."

"That's rough."

"Yeah. Sometimes I think how nice it would be to just leave. But he needs me. Like Mom used to."

His words scared her. She hoped he didn't mean offing himself — especially after what he'd said about wishing his dad had shot him the day of his little sister's accident. She wanted to ask him to sit with her and Audrey, but choked on the words.

He turned to go.

"Wait. Have the cops solved your mom's case yet?" *What are you doing, Kendra?*

"Nope. The last they told Dad was that they're talking to the people who work in the stores where she shopped. Again."

"Oh. Did she have a favorite store?" *Shut up, you idiot.*

"The Trading Post."

Her stupid mouth just kept moving. "How come?"

"Oh, you know, they have all kinds of stuff, old and new, even touristy stuff. Exactly what Mom liked. She could spend hours in there."

"Yeah?"

"Yup. She got to be good friends with the owner, Sam. If she'd find something she liked, but it was the wrong color, he'd order it for her. Lotsa times it was little girls' stuff. He'd even deliver to the farm."

She wondered why the man hadn't shipped the items directly. "That was nice of him. Hey, gotta get goin'. I'm sure the cops will make a breakthrough soon." She headed to the restroom, her mind whirling with this new tidbit. Once again, she was torn.

Back in the bleachers, she tried to block out the chance meeting. But even when the game ended, and Johnny loped over to her, ecstatic with his team's victory, she still saw Alex's sad face in her mind. And when Johnny reached out his hand to her to walk her toward the exit and she felt the familiar attraction charge up her arm, her mind was still a jumble. *It doesn't sound like Alex can talk to his dad. I might be the only person he can confide in.*

In bed that night, her brain searched for why the store owner had delivered orders to Glory. *Maybe shipping was less expensive if he included her order with others delivered to the store. Maybe Glory was afraid her husband would see the tall UPS truck pulling into their driveway and know she was buying more stuff to fill up an already overflowing house. Or maybe — just maybe — they were romantically involved.*

She felt her resolve fading and hated herself for it. But some unknown force pushed at her. *I need to check this guy out,* she thought as she longed for sleep. Finally, she drifted off.

Late the next morning, she told her mom she was going to look for a birthday present for Toni.

"Okay," Mom said. "We'll be at the Laundromat. You know Saturday is laundry and cleaning day so you can spruce up the bathroom when you get back since you won't be around to help me fold clothes."

She grimaced at the thought, but agreed. She headed downtown, hoping she wouldn't see Audrey or Johnny. Then she realized she was being silly. After all, she was just shopping.

Out front, a faded sign read *The Trading Post, Nebraska's Hidden Treasure.* It creaked back and forth on its chains in the breeze. Entering the store, she spotted a man at the checkout counter. She casually walked to the toy section and gave him a sideways look as she passed. *That must be him.*

Toni had been begging for months for a Furby Boom for her fifth birthday. She was glad to find the display of Furbys at the end of an aisle within view of the register where she alternated between looking at the funny little creatures and secretly watching the man as he rang up sales.

He appeared to be fairly young, by grown-up standards anyway. She guessed he was probably in his thirties, but his demeanor seemed much older. He was polite with the shoppers, but something in his manner told a different story. She'd heard working with the public could be a real drag. Maybe he was just worn out. And looking how he did — his face was misshapen — his nose too big and too far to one side of his face — beady eyes under heavy brows ——probably meant he'd have to work even harder to keep customers coming back.

She knew from the photo how beautiful Glory was, and she'd heard on more than one occasion what a terrific personality she had. *He looks like a loser. She would never cheat with this guy.*

Pulling a Furby from the shelf, she walked to the checkout. *So much for getting a cell phone.* She dug in her pocket and peeled off some bills. Mom had helped with a twenty, but this was still a big hit to her savings. Actually, Toni was a little young for it, but like all little kids, she'd caved into the non-stop commercials showing all the neat things it could do. The toy could be named and would then respond when called by its name. It could even talk to other Furbys. It'd laugh when tickled, and you never knew what the funny-looking little thing might say to you. The list of its features went on and on.

Audrey and I need to start mowing lawns again. I need the bucks. As the man greeted her and asked if she'd like a gift box, she watched for any clues that he wasn't what he seemed. But she couldn't find fault with anything he said or did. *Looks like a dead end. But there was something about him that made her uneasy. Was it just her imagination?*

Chapter 25

Deidre hunched over her desk. For the umpteenth time, she picked up the folder with the citizens' tips on the Delgado murder. It was fat and frayed at the edges. She started leafing through them, all the while thinking how something like this brought the strange-os out of the woodwork. Frannie Murdock had called many times and finally visited the precinct unannounced. She was certain the murderer was a spirit of some kind. Deidre reluctantly sat down with the woman. Her police training hadn't prepared her for dealing with people like Mrs. Murdock. She took the only course she thought might work with the woman.

"Mrs. Murdock, I'm so glad we've got conscientious citizens like you. I see my officers have taken down your ideas and I'll keep them in mind as we continue to investigate." She smiled at the woman. "Is there anything else you'd like to add to your statement while you're here?" She knew this would open the flood gates, but hoped that if Murdock felt she'd truly been heard, she'd go back to her other delusions and leave them alone. After listening to the woman's flights of fantasy for fifteen minutes, which seemed like fifteen years, she made her excuses, thanked her profusely, and saw her out of the building.

And then there was Benny Manning. He claimed he'd seen a black SUV, with heavily tinted windows, going up the Delgado drive on the day Glory died. He said there were four men in dark suits in the car. He was convinced it was the mob. When she'd asked how he could see the men and what they were wearing if the windows were tinted, he didn't have an answer.

She kept paging through the folder. Her tired eyes lit on a small piece of paper. It was that Morgan kid's voice mail about finding a sleeping bag in the Delgado hayloft. Of course, the tip hadn't been of any help, but she remembered her intention to pay Kendra a visit. She'd tried to put the fear of God in her before, by threatening jail time, but obviously, that hadn't worked. She needed to squelch this before the kid got herself hurt. *Time to get her mom involved.*

At the rundown apartment building, she located the correct unit number. It was on the lower level. *Good. No stairs. Really gotta get back in shape.* Kendra answered her knock and when she saw Deidre, she looked like she wanted to melt into the floor. "Your mother home?"

Kendra shook her head.

Deidre brushed past her into the tiny living room. Looking around at the meager surroundings, she remembered how the girl's mom had struggled to pay the bills. It was clear nothing had changed. She tamped down the sympathy rising to the surface. "When's she gonna be home?"

"Don't know," Kendra fibbed.

She made herself at home on the sofa. "I'm here about the voice mail lead you left on our phone system."

"That wasn't me." The girl wiped her palms on her jeans.

She leaned her considerable frame forward. "I know it was you. I'll charge you with breaking and entering into the Delgado barn, and before that — their house. You're in such an all-fired hurry to catch criminals that you're becoming one yourself."

The girl seemed to give up the charade and slumped down into a threadbare arm chair. She stared at the floor for a time, then said, "I know better. I *do* know better. Just can't help myself. You must think I'm totally whacked."

She saw tears spring to the girl's eyes. "Hardly." *You've done it this time, scared the kid good. But isn't that what you wanted?*

"My friends say I am," Kendra mumbled.

"Nope. I'd say you just wanna find justice for Glory." She could hardly believe her own words. *Now I'm making excuses for her.*

"Really?"

"Maybe it's your passion," Deidre admitted.

"Passion? Isn't passion something like those artist people have — like musicians?"

"Not necessarily. Could be someone who invents something or starts their own business. Whatever drives a person — that's their passion."

Kendra looked at Diedre as if she'd pulled a St. Bernard through a key hole.

"Personally, I wouldn't be happy doing anything else. Although, right now I'm pretty frustrated."

"Oh?"

"Yeah. You wanna know the truth? Sure, I came here to scare you, but also to distract myself. This investigation is driving me nuts right now." Suddenly a light came on in her brain. "You know, maybe I've been looking at this the wrong way."

"Huh?"

"You were the one that broke Cloud's case for us. Even though you were way too young to be doing what you did, it was like you had a knack for it. Here's an idea. How'd you like to be a police cadet?"

"What?"

"Yeah, you're almost old enough. Usually there's a background check, an interview and a probation period, but I already know you."

"Oh, my gosh! Seriously?"

"Seriously."

Kendra vigorously nodded her head up and down.

"Think your mom will agree? Normally cadets get a special uniform and do ride-alongs with the officers, but you'll be working undercover with me, so no uniform for now. And just so you know — cadets don't get paid — it's strictly volunteer."

"Have a feeling Mom won't let me. Can't we just do it without her knowing?"

"There you go again — plotting away. No. We have to get her permission."

"Well, maybe she'll go for it if she's convinced I'll be totally safe. But I think the kicker would be if she knew I got paid something."

Of course, that would be the carrot that would work. This girl is shrewd beyond her years. "All right. I'll check the budget – it should allow for something. She hauled herself up off the sofa and headed toward the door. "Have your mom call me when she gets home." As she drove back to her office, she thought about what she'd promised. *Oh boy, I probably really screwed up — but I know the girl isn't going to quit snooping around. This way I'll know what she's up to and I can protect her.*

That night Deidre called Joanne and told her the plan.

"Have you lost your mind?" her friend asked.

"Probably. But the kid won't butt out. Plus, she's a natural."

"But what about the liability?"

"It's no different from using a police informant."

"Is, too. She's a minor, you do-do bird."

"I'm aware." But in spite of Joanne's warning, she felt herself liking the idea more and more. "Hey, I'll keep her close under the pretense of working the case together. She'll be safe that way. Hell, what am I saying? We *will* be working together. I'm fresh out of ideas and leads, and young minds think outside the box."

"You're going to be *in* the box if this goes south."

"I know, I know, I know," she said resolutely.

Chapter 26

Kendra couldn't believe it. Mom had actually given permission for her to help Deidre. Of course, Mom knew her from the Grimsby case. *But still. Pretty AH-MAZING!*

She rushed to school to tell Audrey and Johnny. *Would they be mad?*

Audrey's ecstatic response was a welcome relief.

"Seriously? How cool!" Her friend hugged her hard. "Promise to tell me every little thing that happens, okay?"

"I was afraid you'd freak again. 'Course, I'll let you know what's goin' on. I'm just so glad you're down with it." They looked at each other and giggled. Audrey explained that the fact that the law was in the picture made Kendra's involvement in the case, not only acceptable, but enviable.

They rushed to find Johnny before class. She had to fight Audrey for the chance to tell him her news. But instead of congratulating her, he slammed his locker door so hard she thought it would come off the hinges. He stomped away.

"Johnny, wait!" Kendra yelled. She looked wildly at Audrey. "What's happening?"

"Guess he's not as thrilled as we are."

"But why? You think it's great."

"You'll have to ask him. If you can catch him, that is."
Audrey gave her a shove.

She ran through the mob of kids, but Johnny's legs were a
lot longer than hers. The five-minute bell rang for first period
and she knew it was too late to catch him now. She turned and
slouched off to science class. Her next chance would be lunch
time. The morning dragged on forever. She tried to concentrate
on her school work, but the angry look on Johnny's face obliter-
ated her attention span. Finally, noon arrived and she rushed to
the lunch room. He was bent over his food with Audrey and
Lucas in their usual places across the table.

She scooted in beside him. She looked down at the grease
congealing on his pepperoni slice. It made her stomach turn.
"Johnny, what's wrong? I thought you'd be happy. I'll be out
of danger and still able to help with the case."

He moved further down the bench. "Nobody can protect
you 24/7. Is that cop gonna live at your place?"

"'Course not."

"That's what I thought."

"I'll be super-careful. Promise."

He took a huge bite of salad and stared daggers at her. "I
let you talk me into breaking into the Delgado farmhouse —
God, I still can't believe I did that. Then when you heard
about O'Connor, I could see the wheels turning again. Well,
I've had enough. I DO NOT NEED YOUR KIND OF
CRAZY!"

There was something steely in his voice she hadn't heard
before. *He's breaking up with me. No, no, no!* She grabbed her
backpack and ran, tears streaming down her hot cheeks. At

first, she didn't know where she was, only that she was pushing past kids who stared at her like she was a zombie. The news would be all over school by the end of the day. She found herself in the girls' bathroom, sobbing into a scratchy paper towel. Someone put an arm around her shoulder — Audrey.

"It's okay. He'll get over it."

"Don't think so. He's awful mad," she mumbled around the towel. "And I can't figure why."

"Yeah, does seem strange. Maybe it's about more than your safety."

"What?"

"Could be jealous. Might be thinking you won't have time for him now," Audrey said. "Who knows? Guys are a whole different animal. Come on, let's get you some lunch far away from that Neanderthal."

"Nah. Can't go back in there. I'm goin' home." She knew her straight-arrow friend would never skip school and that was fine. She wanted to be alone anyway.

"'K, I'll call you tonight." Audrey gave her another hug.

She gave her cheeks a last swipe with the towel and left through the back exit. As she walked, she replayed the horrible scene in her head. *Maybe Audrey's right — he's jealous. After all, it wasn't that long ago that Audrey was jealous of Johnny. So, she definitely knows what she's talking about.*

At home, she dumped her backpack and crawled into the comfort of her bed. She buried her head under the covers and cried some more. Grabbing her old MP3 player, she let the tunes of her favorite artists wash over her — Brad Paisley, Rihanna and Alicia Keys. As Rihanna's "Diamonds," played, she held her pillow to her chest. She knew other girls who threw pity parties for themselves and she'd always thought they were being babies. Now she was one of them. *I was wrong to judge.*

She lay there for a long time wallowing in her heartache. Then one of her favorite songs came through her earbuds. She realized that the artist was singing about her. The lyrics were about a girl whose world is falling apart, but she knows that she's strong enough to overcome whatever happens. She found herself singing along.

Suddenly, she felt better. Yanking back the covers, she stood and announced to the empty room, "Too bad, Johnny. If you can't stand a strong girl, then you're right to break up with me." She'd heard somewhere that even if you didn't feel a certain way, that if you acted like you did, it would eventually be true. She knew she wouldn't be over Johnny for a long, long time. *But I refuse to let him or anyone else see how he hurt me.* She hurried to the kitchen for a snack before she went to pick up Toni.

Chapter 27

"**I**'ll be at your place in five minutes. Wait in the parking lot," Deidre said. When she arrived, she found a gloomy-looking Kendra waiting at the curb.

"Hi Chief Goodwin," she mumbled as she fastened her seat belt.

"You're my assistant now, so no need to be so formal. Call me: 'Chief,' or 'Deidre.'" She launched into what was on her mind. "I'm sure you heard about that farmer's death. I'm trying to figure out if there's any connection with the Delgado murder." She looked at Kendra for a response, but got none. "What's wrong with you? I expected you'd be all hyped — your first day and all."

The girl slouched in her seat. "I am. I'm really happy."

"Don't look like it to me. Anything to do with boys?" When the girl didn't answer, she figured she was right and decided to shut up. Kendra would tell her later if she wanted to. She let a few minutes pass while she drove and sipped on her coffee. "We're going over to Fremont to talk to O'Connor's ex. Let me re-phrase that — you're waiting in the cruiser while I talk to her."

The mid-size town of Fremont was a couple of hours away, and they rode in silence except for an occasional blast from the car radio. Once, Bianca's voice crackled over the air waves to let Deidre know nothing exciting was happening back at home base. Another time it was Chucky asking what time they were expected back. As they drew nearer to Mrs. O'Connor's house, Kendra seemed to perk up. By the time they pulled up in front of the white two-story clapboard, she saw the girl was her old self.

"Can I come in, too? Please?"

"No way. Wait here — come tell me if there any radio calls." She was 99.9% sure there wouldn't be any. She'd instructed Bianca to ring her cell if anything important came up. But Kendra didn't need to know that. She left the wide-eyed girl playing with the radio buttons and walked to the door.

A worn-looking, middle-aged woman answered the bell and invited Deidre into the dining room. The house was clean and well cared for, but that care didn't extend to Mrs. O'Connor herself. Her graying hair was carelessly pulled back in a ponytail and her T-shirt was covered in what looked like grease stains. They'd no sooner sat down than the woman launched into her grievances. "That tight bastard," she said. "I put up with him for years. He'd leave post-it notes all over the house."

"Post-it notes?" She placed her recorder on the table. "You don't mind if I tape this, do you?"

"No problem," the woman said. "Yeah, Post-its — like on the thermostat. 'Don't forget who pays the electric bill.' Or on the washer. 'Hot water ain't free, 'ya know.' Or in the refrigerator on my daughter's pudding cups. 'Could save money if you weren't too lazy to cook this yourself.'" The former Mrs. O'Connor shook her head. "That last one made me so mad I went on strike. Quit doing his laundry and meals."

She nodded for her to go on.

"Things got real bad after that. He started sleeping in the spare bedroom. Didn't talk unless we absolutely had to. The last straw was when Margi got real sick with a 105-degree fever. He didn't want to spend money on the doctor. I took her in anyway. When she was well enough, I packed us up and never looked back."

"Did he ever get violent with you?"

"No, at least he kept his big mitts to himself." The woman continued on, uttering more complaints, but merely more variations about how frugal her husband had been.

Finally, she stood and punched 'Stop' on the recorder. "Well, thank you for your time. You've given me some good information here."

Back in the cruiser, she played the interview for Kendra, who not surprisingly, asked a million questions. *Inquisitive mind. Good for police work. It's a wonder that she waited out here.*

What she didn't know was that Kendra had snuck out of the car a few minutes after she saw Deidre disappear inside. She'd gone up the sidewalk and turned toward the side of the house. A gray cat lying beneath a bush had given them both a fright. She watched the cat go flying from its sleeping place and took a deep breath to steady herself. She tiptoed on until she heard voices coming from an open window. Peering over the window sill, she saw Deidre and a woman seated at a table.

Unfortunately, she heard only bits and pieces of the conversation over her loudly beating heart. When the chief rose to leave, she ran like crazy and was back in the cruiser before she was discovered.

"So, what's our next step?" Kendra asked as Deidre stowed the recorder in the glove box.

"Head back to the office. I wish I'd just called O'Connor's ex instead. She really didn't tell me anything I didn't already know, except that he never physically hurt her, or the daughter. That's good info, but we already knew he was a skin flint from what his neighbors told us."

"So, what about the daughter — shouldn't we talk to her, too?"

"She's at a friend's." Deidre thought about it as she pulled away from the curb. She hated talking to kids after they'd lost a parent. But dammit, Kendra was right. She pulled over and called Mrs. O'Connor. "Would you mind if we talked to your daughter?"

"Don't think she'll be any help. Margi and her dad weren't close, but go ahead. She's over at Justine's house." The woman's tone was begrudging, but she gave her the address and said she'd call over to give her daughter a heads-up.

When they arrived, they saw a girl sitting on the top step of the porch. "That must be her," Deidre said. As the girl sauntered up to the vehicle, she noted her piercings and tatts. "Hi, you're Margi? I'm Chief Goodwin, and this is Kendra. Why don't you jump in the back? This won't take long."

Kendra bolted out of the car and climbed in the back seat with the girl.

What is she up to? She considered putting her in her place, but something stopped her.

"We were hoping you could tell us a little about your dad? By the way, sorry for your loss," Kendra said.

"Ain't you a little young to be hangin' with the law?" Margi looked Kendra up and down.

"Guess so. Been through some heavy-duty stuff with the chief a while back. She thinks that deserves a ride-along."

"Humph."

Margi's tone was so defiant that Deidre was sure they wouldn't get anything out of her. She could tell the girl was a couple of years older than Kendra and in a whole different stratosphere. She reminded her of the many Goth kids she'd seen on the streets of Omaha. Dressed all in black, the sallow complexions, cigarette and marijuana smoke wafting from their clothes. No doubt she believed Kendra was just a little nerd troublemaker. *And, of course, the little twerp's refusing to make eye contact with me so I can warn her off. I'm sure she knows I'm furious.* She watched as the girl turned and blurted out, "Would you mind telling us how you got along with your dad?"

A strange look passed over Margi's face. "Why are you really here? Cops don't go to all this trouble for suicides." She hugged herself. "You don't think he killed himself, do you?" Before either of them could answer, the girl's tough exterior dissolved. She hunched over and began to cry.

This is exactly why I hate talking to kids. I can handle adults breaking down, but not this. She saw Kendra move closer to Margi, and drape her arm around her heaving shoulders. "I'm so sorry. We didn't mean to upset you," Deidre said, handing some tissues over the seat.

Kendra patted Margi's arm. "You don't have to talk about it if you don't want to. But it would really help us."

"People said my dad wasn't a very nice man. Mom hated him." She rubbed her eyes, smearing her heavy black mascara. "But he was always nice to me. When I was little, he never spanked me — not once — no matter how rotten I was."

"Did you see him much after you moved away?" Kendra asked.

"Once a month. He never missed. We'd go to a movie, or shopping, or whatever. If there was something I really wanted to do, he'd make sure it happened. He even took me to a Bruno Mars concert in Lincoln."

"Sweet."

"Yeah, it was way cool." Margi swiped at her tears again and moved to go. "That's all I gotta say."

Deidre was surprised at the girl's sudden departure, but recovered in time to say, "Hey, thanks for talking to us. You've been a huge help." As they watched the girl slump back to her friend's house, she turned a cold eye on Kendra. "Kinda full of yourself, huh?"

"Sorry, chief. I thought she might talk to someone more her own age. Won't happen again." She made the sign of an "x" over her heart.

"See that it doesn't!" After she'd allowed a minute for her words to sink in, she said, "Well, the ex-wife and daughter sure have different opinions of the guy. Not all that uncommon though. Looks to me like O'Connor was a jerk to everyone except Margi, but I still can't figure what he did that was so bad that it got him murdered."

As they drove back to Finchville, Deidre thought about how her junior detective had gotten the tough-looking teen to open up. She'd never admit it to Kendra, but she was pretty impressed.

Chapter 28

Kendra tried to focus on her grammar paper. She diagrammed the first sentence, but her concentration dissolved before the second. *School's such a waste of time when there are murders to be solved.*

And then there's Johnny. He was always there at the back of her mind. Rumors were rampant that he was into Shania Webb. *Whenever he sees me at school, he looks the other way. Is that why?*

Mom had said she could invite a few of her friends to Toni's birthday party. She'd already invited Audrey, Lucas, and Alex. She wanted to ask Johnny, but how could she, when he obviously didn't want to speak to her?

Her thoughts seesawed back to the first murder. She ran through the facts in her mind. It was common knowledge in town that the police had cleared Glory's husband, brother-in-law, and two homeless guys. But since the woman was known to feed the down-and-out, there was still a chance a different one had killed her and was now long gone. That was the popular theory among the citizenry since no one wanted to believe one of their neighbors could do such a horrible thing.

The chief had told her Glory hadn't been sexually assaulted and the only injury to her body had been the wounds to her head. Also, that Ricky Delgado didn't think anything had been stolen, but it was difficult to tell, given the condition of the house. That brought her thoughts to the photo she'd lifted — *thank goodness something that small won't be missed.*

Then there was the O'Connor case. Deidre had told her about the man brazenly admitting his hatred of Latinos. And even before he'd been found hanging from a rafter in his barn, the chief had suspected that Glory's death might be a hate crime. So, when the medical examiner told Deidre he doubted the man had done himself in, she believed the two deaths were definitely connected. The chief was sure that if they could solve Glory's murder, O'Connor's killer would be exposed, too. But without any new leads, the cases were rapidly growing cold.

Kendra realized she was getting a headache racking her brain and coming up with no good ideas about the murders, so she let her daydreams flit back to Johnny. She missed him so much. Her skin tingled as she remembered the way she felt when he held her close. She imagined snuggling in his arms and how he would nuzzle her neck. She brushed her hand gently over her lips.

"Hey."

She was jarred back to reality by the boy sitting in front of her.

"Got an eraser I can borrow?" He was turned in his seat and looking at her expectantly.

She fumbled in her backpack and handed him a pink Pearl eraser. "Need it back when class is over," she whispered.

"You're the girls who's working with the cops, ain't ya?" he muttered back.

"Yeah, so?" Kendra stared at him. He turned away. *Did he think she was weird or cool?* She just wanted to be a normal kid. Her gaze shifted to one of the popular girls in the next row. *I know I'll never be like her and her cheerleader friends, with their long straight hair and legs that don't quit. And for sure I'm not a geek. But I'm not a misfit, either. I finally had a really cool boyfriend. And now I've lost him. Just because I want to find a killer. Not fair.*

There was a lull in Deidre's day — she hated that — it meant she was fresh out of new information to act on in the investigations. She stuffed down her frustration with a blueberry muffin, and then turned to stare out the window behind her. *Got to do something.* She swiveled her chair and grabbed her phone. "Kendra, got some time this afternoon?"

"Yeah, homework's done and Mom's here with my sister."

"Good. Pick you up in a few." *The kid is interested in police work. May as well teach her something.* "Be gone a while, Bianca," she called as she headed out of the station.

Kendra was waiting in her usual spot in the apartment parking lot. "Where we headed?" she asked as she fastened her seat belt.

Deidre pointed the cruiser toward the edge of town. "Take a guess."

"We're not headed in the direction of either of the victims' farms or downtown — so — no clue."

"What we're doing is SOP."

"SOP?"

"Standard operating procedure," she replied. "A lot of this stuff is pretty boring, but sometimes it pays off."

"We're going to Holy Names Cemetery?" Kendra asked as the car turned and passed under a wrought iron arch with peeling paint, featuring the graveyard's name at its apex. There were tall weeds at the base of the arch, but the rest of the cemetery was mown down to the dirt.

She heard the amazement in her cadet's voice. She laughed. "Sometimes killers visit the graves of their victims."

"Why?"

"Different reasons, depending on their motives. For psychopaths, it's a way to relive the experience. They get off on the kill all over again. Damned sickos. Others regret what they've done and their guilt gets the best of them." They got out of the car and walked together through the rows of graves. She noticed the girl kept her head down, not looking at the inscriptions on the headstones. Then she remembered it hadn't been that long since her friend's burial in this very graveyard. *Gotta be rough on the kid.* She suddenly stopped and Kendra bumped into her.

"Sorry."

"Here it is." Deidre pointed at a pink marble headstone: *Glory Delgado, Loving Wife and Mother, January 3, 1975 - April 2, 2014.* The earth around the marker was still fresh. A spray of red carnations and baby's breath rested in the little metal holder at its base.

"How often do you come out here?"

"Two or three times a week. Actually, I was here when Ricky Delgado brought these flowers the other day. Hold up. What's this?" Her eyes fell on something small tucked behind the bouquet. She pulled a tissue from her pocket and carefully picked it up. She turned it over to get a better look. It was a little jewelry-making kit, the kind with large, colorful beads and heavy string — perfect for a small child.

Kendra eyes were huge. "Why would *that* be here?"

"Exactly." She pointed at a gravesite with a small marker next to Glory's. "Ricky moved his daughter's remains here to be close to her mother. If he'd brought this, he would've placed it on Sophia's grave, not his wife's."

"So, what does it mean?"

"Our killer was here — that's what it means. And he knew that Glory bought things for her dead daughter."

"Wow!"

"Now we know for sure this wasn't a random crime. The killer knew Glory, and my guess is he feels guilty about what he did. Come on, gotta get this to the crime lab right now."

Even though Kendra seemed excited about the discovery, it was plain she was shaken by the sight of the mother and daughter gravesites. *Good,* she thought, *maybe she'll realize this is serious business and won't try anything stupid.*

A week had passed with Deidre calling the crime lab daily about the beading kit until the director finally lost patience.

"I know you've got a hot case but believe it or not, we've got a backlog here. If I didn't know how to prioritize, I wouldn't have this job. So, relax. We'll let you know the second we get your results."

When the call finally came several days later, the news put her into a deep funk. No fingerprints. No DNA.

While she'd been waiting, she'd talked to the Delgado family and the town's shopkeepers again. No one admitted to leaving the kit on Glory's grave. With the toy's discovery, her gut said this death wasn't about race. Most murders were fueled by love, hate or money. Glory was an attractive woman, plus everyone said she oozed charisma. They hadn't turned up any evidence of an affair, but what if someone wanted one, and Glory didn't? A stalker. They could be extremely dangerous — often delusional — and intelligent. *A bad combination.*

Time for one last ploy. "Bianca, come here a sec." When her assistant stuck her bee-hived head in the door, she said, "I need everybody here for a meeting — ASAP —including the kid — Kendra."

Bianca looked surprised. "What's up?"

"Just do it."

The woman popped her gum and held her ground.

"Time to shake things up. Somebody knows something about these murders and we're gonna find that somebody. Now get on it."

A little while later, six expectant faces stared at her from the other side of her desk as she wrote on a legal tablet. Finally, Chucky asked, "What's going on, chief?"

Deidre scribbled a minute more on the paper in front of her. "A town meeting over at the Grange. Tomorrow night. That'll give us time to get the word out. And I want you all there."

"Even me?" Bianca squeaked. "What for?"

"I'm sure the killer will want to know what's going on and show up. Plus, someone might come forward with new information. I need you all there while I'm conducting the meeting to watch for anyone acting suspicious — pay close attention to body language. You'll sit at a table at the front of the room where you can have eyes on everyone, except for Kendra. No need to advertise that she's helping us. We'll station her in the back somewhere."

"Body language?" Kendra asked.

"Yeah. Like, if someone seems nervous," Deidre replied. "Maybe someone's tapping his foot, or crossing his legs."

"Crossing his legs?" The girl looked mystified.

"If someone's trying to hide something, the person might cross his arms or legs, or both. It's an unconscious response that reveals a need to protect himself and his secret. Cops call them 'tells' and there are tons of 'em. I'll go over some of the more obvious ones with you and Bianca ahead of time."

The chief picked up the paper she'd been writing on and handed it to Bianca. "Make up the meeting notices — here's a rough draft. As soon they're ready, I want everyone, except Kendra, to post them all around town, pronto! I don't wanna see a bare telephone pole anywhere."

As they rose to go, Chucky asked, "How much you gonna tell the town about the cases?"

"Just enough to scare up a murderer."

Chapter 29

As people filed into Grange Hall the following evening, the room sizzled with excitement. Kendra watched from her seat near the back. True to the chief's instructions, her staff sat at a table in the front, with the exception of Chucky, who was stationed at the entry door. She struggled to remember what Deidre had told her about body language. *Man, they all look edgy. Even Pearl, the nice old lady who owns the boutique, looks like she's having a nervous breakdown.* According to the old-timers, there'd never been an emergency town meeting as long as they'd walked the planet. To her, the tension in the air felt like a swarm of buzzing bees.

Fifteen minutes before the meeting was due to begin, every chair was filled. People continued to straggle in, finding places to stand at the sides and back of the room. The fire chief frowned and walked over to where Deidre sat with her crew. She watched as he bent to talk to her. Her curiosity got the best of her and she made her way over to Chucky. "What's that all about?"

"He's probably got his panties in a bunch 'cuz we're over the limit of bodies allowed. We're breaking the fire code."

"Great."

"Don't worry. Chief will get her way." His eyes scanned the room. "Better go back to your seat."

At seven o'clock sharp, Deidre rose and looked around the room. The scraping of chairs, the hum of conversation, and even the cries of a baby stopped, as if on cue. It was so quiet that when a single cough broke the silence, it sounded like a sonic boom. "I want to thank all of you for turning out tonight. I know some of you drove in from your farms and I really appreciate it. I'll keep this short so you can be home by a decent hour."

"Unless you've been living under a rock, you know we've had two mysterious deaths in the area recently." She waited for a few nervous chuckles to subside. "I'm glad to report we've ruled out a lot of suspects. But we've hit a dead end, so the department needs your help." As she spoke, she scanned the crowd. "I know someone knows something. You may not know that you know, but you do." She gestured at her head. "Think about it. Maybe go home and sleep on it. Then call or come in. If you want to remain anonymous — no problem." Again, her eyes searched the room. She waited a moment for her words to sink in. "Now, I'll take a few questions."

The room exploded with noise. Some jumped to their feet while others waved their hands. "Okay, take it easy! Sit down and we'll do this in an orderly way. Keep in mind, I can't answer everything, but I'll do the best I can." She pointed to a young man with a toddler in his lap. "Yes?"

"You mentioned you don't have any suspects, but how about persons of interest?"

"Oh, I forgot to mention," Deidre said, "please identify yourself. I know a lot of you, but not everyone."

"Roy Seifert," the man replied.

"Mr. Seifert, I can't give you any names right now. I can tell you we've ruled out all of the family members of both victims. We've also cleared the two vagrants who had been at the Delgado farm. However, there may be other homeless people we don't know about. If anyone here is aware of any, please let us know."

"Also, you may've heard the gossip around town that the murders are related to hate crimes. I haven't ruled this out as a possibility." Kendra saw the chief pause and look hard at Zach Mortensen. She knew this was the bigot Deidre had interviewed before O'Connor's death. All eyes turned to him. Instead of looking embarrassed, he glared back at her. "Again, I urge you to report anything along those lines — it could be something in the past — something small — it doesn't matter. Give us the information and we'll decide what's important."

Kendra trembled inside as she saw the man's hateful stare. She couldn't believe how calm Deidre seemed. The chief ignored him and pointed at another raised hand. Kendra glanced at the back of the room and saw Chucky standing tall and looking ready for anything. None of her friends were here — not even Alex — but even though she was scared, she still loved every second of this drama. *Maybe Johnny's right. Maybe I am weird. But if this is what weird feels like, I'm all in!*

Next, Diedre selected a woman in the middle of the room. "Ida Plumley here. Was Mrs. Delgado — um — you know?" The woman turned red.

Deidre looked at Ricky Delgado in the first row and Kendra saw him wince at the question. She knew if the chief didn't answer, the town would believe Glory had been raped, so she wasn't surprised when she answered truthfully while giving Ricky an apologetic look. "No, Mrs. Delgado was not sexually assaulted. Cause of death was a blow to the head."

"Yes?" Deidre quickly moved to the next person.

"I'm Herb McCoy. What about forensics?"

"I can't say too much about that, other than we've collected DNA and blood work from both scenes. However," Deidre paused and searched the faces before her, "we do have some new fingerprints the crime lab is processing. They were found on an item left at Mrs. Delgado's gravesite."

Murmurs rocketed around the hall at this news.

The chief's face was a blank slate. Kendra was amazed that the woman could lie so convincingly.

"Quiet, please!" Deidre said, as she motioned to a woman across the aisle. "What's your question, ma'am?"

"Hi, I'm Sally Hargis. I heard the killings were part of a satanic ritual." The woman had coal black hair, dark red lips and nails, and tattoos covering her neck and arms. She was dressed all in black.

A collective gasp went up in the room. Kendra felt certain that if there were such a ritual, this woman would be at the center of it.

Sally Hargis looked around, as if in surprise, but she caught a glimmer of a smile playing across her lips. While most people were either angry or fearful, this woman seemed to relish the shock she was causing. *It's as if she can't get enough of bad things happening in the world. She's creepy.*

Deidre gave the woman a withering look and said, "I don't know where you heard that, but there's not a speck of truth to it. I can see this dialogue is deteriorating so that's enough for tonight. But remember to think about any tips you may have. Nothing's too small. I intend to solve these crimes, and I need your help to do it."

Disappointment showed on many faces at the abrupt end to the meeting, but the room was abuzz with what had transpired. People talked excitedly as they headed toward the exit and out into the warm night. The chief made her way over to where Bianca sat.

She hurried to the front of the room in time to hear Bianca ask the chief, "How come you didn't allow time for new tips?"

"I'd rather they come in separately — protects their identity and gives us a chance for a thorough interview. Be ready for a busy day tomorrow. And first thing in the morning, I want you to run a check on this Sally Hargis person."

"You don't think she did it, do you?" Bianca asked.

"Not likely. At least not by herself, but check her out anyway." Then she raised her voice to all of her staff. "Everyone hang around a few minutes. We'll meet in the kitchen after they've cleared out. Need to know if you saw anything interesting."

Chapter 30

He raised the wine glass to his lips, but tasted nothing. He stared at the blank TV screen. *Fingerprints? How could there be fingerprints on the bead kit? I wore gloves when I went out to the cemetery. I know I was super-careful. That lady cop lied — she's trying to bait me. Unless...shit! When I unpacked the shipment last month. Could've gotten my fingerprints on it then. You dumb S.O.B.*

He shifted in his chair and wracked his brain for a solution. *With any luck, the prints they've got are from some kid pawing it. But what if they ARE my prints? How can I lie myself out of it?* He took another gulp of the Chardonnay.

Suddenly, he smiled. *Hell, what am I thinking? Won't have to explain a damned thing. As the store owner, my prints could legitimately be on the kit. Get a grip.* He took a deep breath and relaxed.

His thoughts drifted to the times he'd followed Glory home, but just kept going when she turned in her long driveway. She wouldn't have understood. She'd made that crystal clear the one time he'd shown up unannounced and pretended the pair of sunglasses he held belonged to her.

"Why, you know those aren't mine. You sold me the ones I have just last week and they look nothing like that." She'd given him a funny look.

He knew then he'd have to be more careful. A few times when she was in town, he'd hung the "Closed" sign on the shop door and surreptitiously left little notes on her windshield. He'd watched her from a distance when she returned to her car and read them, a warm feeling growing in his belly and the lyrics from Sting's old song running through his head:

Every move you make,
Every step you take,
I'll be watching you....

She'd lifted her head and looked carefully around. Each time, she'd crumpled the note and tossed it on the ground. A part of him had withered, but then he'd consoled himself with the notion that she just didn't realize how much he cared. Somehow, he'd make her understand.

But now, in the silence of his living room, he wondered if anyone had seen him place the notes on her car. Or, if someone had spotted him on his visits to the farm. He tried to remember how many times he'd been out there — too many to count. If so, he knew they'd run right to that cop. *Maybe they already have. Damn, I hate this pissy town and the nosy, small-minded people in it. If only I could get a store in Lincoln, or Omaha, or even Kansas City. Could get away from these idiots. But I can't leave now. That would have guilt written all over it.*

Chapter 31

In the days following the town meeting, Deidre and her staff were flooded with calls and walk-ins. The tips had ranged from some that sounded useful to a few really whacked-out ones.

Sitting before her now was a Mrs. Burnham, who claimed she'd seen a man in a long cape, as she walked along the road to take her neighbor some freshly-baked cinnamon rolls. The chief knew the woman lived near the Delgado farm. *Could there be anything to her report?* When Deidre asked her why she hadn't come in sooner, Burnham looked her straight in the eye and exclaimed, "I was too afraid. You would've been too, if you'd seen his face. He walked straight towards me on the shoulder of the road, and leered at me. It was the evilest grin I've ever seen in my entire life!"

"Would you be able to help with a sketch of this guy?"

"Oh my, yes." She smoothed a wayward curl away from her flushed face.

Deidre left the woman with one of her officers who had an artistic flair. Fifteen minutes passed, and she went back to check on their progress. As she approached, the officer looked up at her and covertly rolled his eyes. When she looked over his shoulder at the drawing, she suppressed the urge to laugh. It was the standard likeness many people thought of when they visualized the devil — right down to the horns, tail, and of course, the cape. She managed to hang onto her composure and thanked her for coming in.

The woman clutched her purse to her chest, as if to fend off the demon, and rose to go. "Will you let me know if you find him?"

"Absolutely." Deidre escorted her to the exit as quickly as possible.

So, the department had gone through the motions, checking out every tip and lead. Nothing useful materialized. The Hargis woman, who had piqued Deidre's interest at the town meeting, was checked out and cleared. She'd conducted some questionable cult-like practices, but nothing illegal. However, the clincher was that she had solid alibis for the days of both murders.

The chief was especially disappointed that the false information she'd given about finding fingerprints on the beading kit hadn't scared the killer into betraying himself. *I'm sure he must've been there — he must be one cool customer.* She reflected on the meeting for the hundredth time. No one had stood out to her, or to her crew. *Even Kendra didn't notice anyone out of the ordinary and that girl's sharp, no doubt about it.*

She'd given her a ride home after the meeting and quizzed her again to be sure the young sleuth hadn't picked up on anything.

"I'm sorry. I wish I'd seen something," she'd said. "There were lots of nervous people, but I think they were acting that way 'cuz they're afraid there's a killer in town."

"Yeah, you're probably right." Deidre decided to change the subject. "So, how're things going with you?"

"What?"

"Just wondering how you are. You do have a life besides helping me, right?"

"Oh. Yeah, everything's cool. School's okay. And Mom's doin' good, now that Dad's finally outta here."

Keeping her voice casual, she said, "That's great. Still hanging with that boy you were sweet on last winter?" She glanced over at Kendra's face, but couldn't see her expression in the dim light from the dashboard.

"Johnny?"

"Yeah."

"I was. Turns out he doesn't like me doin' this stuff."

"How come?"

"He's afraid I'll get hurt."

"That *is* a definite possibility, you know."

"But you said you'd keep me safe."

"And I will, as long as you don't do something foolish."

"Do you think I'm weird for wanting to help?"

Deidre laughed. "You're asking the wrong person. I'm just like you — can't stand to see murderers on the loose. Looks to me like you'll be in law enforcement of some kind when you grow up."

"Really?"

"Really."

"My mom's sister works homicides for the Phoenix Police Department. I've only met her a few times so I don't know much about her, but maybe it runs in the family."

"That explains a lot. Looks like your snoopiness is genetic." She chuckled again. "How tall are you?"

Kendra pulled herself up in the passenger seat. "Five-two. Why?"

She heard the surprise in the girl's voice. "I'm pretty sure there are height requirements at the police training center, but even if there aren't, you might have trouble getting over on some of the big bruisers we bust. Looks like you weigh 90 pounds on a good day. If I were you, I'd start eating my Wheaties." She could feel Kendra's stare in the dark car. *It probably hasn't occurred to her that her size could affect her career. Her self-confidence is way, way bigger than she is.*

"What do you mean?" the girl asked after a moment's silence.

"I mean eating healthy — lots of protein and fruits and veggies. And working out — build up your core strength and stamina. But you know, there are other areas of law enforcement. Like, you could be a district attorney and put criminals away after we nail them."

"Nope. I like figuring out who did the crime and bustin' 'em."

"Okay then. Come down to the station after school and I'll get you started on a workout program. And, who knows, if you begin eating right, you may even grow a couple inches."

Deidre was glad the girl was excited about police work, but hearing her talk this way reminded her that she needed to keep a handle on this little whirlwind. Gruffly, she said, "So, like your ex-boyfriend, my goal is to keep you safe. Remember, you're not doing anything on your own."

"Hey, after what I went through with gettin' kidnapped and all, you can't seriously think I'd do somethin' crazy."

Even though Kendra sounded convincing, she remembered all the times the girl had put herself in danger on the Grimsby case. Sure, she's matured some, but an old cliché ran through her head, "A leopard never changes its spots."

A few weeks after the meeting, the tips had trickled down to zero, with nothing to show for the time and effort spent. Deidre was further frustrated that she hadn't been able to locate the man's cologne she'd detected at the Delgado crime-scene. She'd interviewed every man in town, hoping to get a whiff of the fragrance. Maybe she was wrong — maybe the killer didn't live around here.

Weeks turned into months and the cases were growing cold. She'd been over the files so often that she felt she'd worn her fingerprints away. She'd even pulled cold cases from all the surrounding areas, looking for any similarities.

When the Delgado family realized there were no new developments in the case, Alex had helped his dad set up a Facebook Page. The boy made frequent posts. He implored people to come forward with any information. Deidre logged on to the site often to see if any suspicious comments appeared. Once again, she gazed at the photos of a beautiful Glory on the Profile page and was filled with anxiety and frustration. *All right — since I'm at a dead end anyway — I'll give folks the impression the investigation is closed. Maybe the killer will get careless if he thinks we've moved on.*

She left her office and stopped by Pearl's Boutique.

After they'd chatted a bit, the elderly woman asked what was really on her mind. "So, what's happening with your investigation. I heard you had a lot of tips."

"Unfortunately, none of them panned out, so we're putting the cases on the back burner. I think whoever's responsible is long gone by now." She left with the satisfaction of knowing the news would be all over town by nightfall.

Chapter 32

How can six little kids make so much noise? Kendra won-dered. "Okay, everybody, sit in a circle. The birth-day girl's going to open her presents." She pointed to the floor, hoping they'd plant their little butts down. She knew they heard her yell over the din, but they went on acting crazy — blowing on their party horns — doing their best to pop their balloons — and running everywhere. Mom was in the kitchen finishing up the cake, so she couldn't ask her to help, but at least Alex, Audrey and Lucas had showed up. Actually, Audrey and Lucas weren't much use — they only had eyes for each other. It made her all the more aware that Johnny wasn't here. Even though Lucas had said he'd pass along her invite, she hadn't really expected him to show. But,— it still hurt.

Alex plopped himself down on the carpet. Turned out, he was a kid magnet — the four girls and two boys suddenly stopped tearing around the room and wedged themselves as close to him as they could. "Okay, Toni. Which one are you going to open first?" he asked.

She sat back, marveled at the quiet, and watched Toni's delight in her first real birthday party. When her sister tore the wrappings from the Furby Boom, she squealed and hugged it to her. "Thank you Ken'ra!"

Her reaction made her feel good about delaying her plan to buy a cell phone. "You're welcome, little Munchketeer."

Toni was so involved with checking out the Furby that she forgot about her other packages. Finally, at Alex's urging, she tore into her other gifts. When the last present was opened, she thanked all her friends, and they trooped into the kitchen. Her eyes grew wide at the oversized candle in the shape of a number five resting smack in the middle of the cake. Mom directed her to make a wish and blow out the candle. She scrunched her eyes shut and got such a look of concentration, that they all laughed.

As soon as the birthday song was sung and she helped serve the cake and ice cream, Teresa said, "If you and your friends wanna go out to the common area, I've got this."

"Thanks, Mom. I'll be back to help clean up in a bit." Together they hurried out of the apartment carrying paper plates of melting ice cream and chocolate cake. Audrey and Lucas found a small bench for the two of them and she motioned Alex to another one across from the rusty swing set. "Am I glad to get away from that racket! My ears are still ringing."

"Yeah, they were pretty excited," Alex said. He dug into his cake. "Was fun though."

"Glad you were here to help out. Don't have the knack for it like you do." *I guess I'll chance it. I hope I don't upset him like I did at the grocery store.* "So, how're you doing? Still missing your mom?"

Alex stopped mid-bite. "I'll always miss her."

"Sorry." She toyed with her Rocky Road ice cream. "That was a stupid thing to ask."

"S'okay. Nobody else ever brings her up. It's like she never existed."

"I'm sure they don't think that. Probably don't wanna make you sad."

"But I wanna talk about her. Even if it hurts. I don't want people to forget her. If they can forget her, that means I can, too."

She saw the haunted look in his eyes and searched for the right words. "You can talk to me — anytime. Whaddya like to remember about her?"

He was quiet a minute. "After school was our time together. Dad was usually out in the fields, or in the barn. Her favorite spot was the rocker on the porch. She could hear the whir of the windmill blades there. She always said that it calmed her mind."

"Would she just be sittin' there?"

"Oh, no. She'd be doin' somethin' — like shelling peas or mending a shower cap."

"Mending a shower cap?"

"Yup. You know. Like those cheap ones you get at motels?"

"She'd actually take the time to do that?" She tried to keep the amazement from her voice.

Alex shrugged. "Part of the hoarding. She couldn't stand to toss anything. She'd spend hours on stuff like that. Guess that's why she could never catch up. But I liked it 'cuz we'd talk — it was our time together, just the two of us."

For once, she was speechless. Then the detective in her kicked in. "Was she lonely?"

"Nah. She had us. And she went into town even though Dad didn't like it. And like I told you before, Sam would sometimes bring her somethin' she'd ordered from him."

"Would he stay long?"

"Nope. But it gave her somethin' to look forward to."

"But no neighbors would visit?"

"She didn't encourage that. Said women could be judgmental about messy housekeeping."

Later on, after all the commotion from the party had died down, and they were all in bed, she went over Alex's conversation in her mind. *This is the second time he's brought up this Sam guy. I wonder if Deidre's checked him out? Didn't see anything strange that day I sized him up at his store, but maybe I should let her know what Alex said.* She untangled the sheet from her legs and sprawled on her bed, wishing for some relief from the humid spring night.

I know if I were in Alex's place I'd not only want people to remember my mom, but to solve her murder, too. Deidre's cleared his dad, but I wonder about that. Maybe he's just careful about covering his tracks. It wasn't a stretch to imagine such a scenario. She'd seen her own dad use Mom for a punching bag plenty of times and had heard stories of husbands who killed their wives in a rage. Her heart constricted as some of those old scenes of Dad terrorizing them played through her mind. *I'm so glad Mom finally stood up to him. She's still not 100% okay, but that ugly rash on her arms the doctor said was from nerves has disappeared. Just wish she didn't have to work so many hours.* Dad had always been good at staying one step ahead of the child support people and that hadn't changed.

Got to think of something else or I'll never get to sleep. Automatically, her mind drifted to Johnny. She knew he was avoiding her. Truth be told, she'd been doing the same. She didn't know what to say to him. Part of her knew she was better off without him, but the other part longed to be with him again. She loved it when he brushed her hair back from her cheeks with his farm-calloused hands and lifted her chin for a kiss. She thought back to the school's Winter Wonderland Sock Hop when they'd first met over a year ago, and wished for him to hold her as he had that night on the dance floor.

As sleep finally enveloped her, she was vaguely aware of her subconscious telling her a plan for Sam Edelson.

Chapter 33

The next morning Alex's remark about the guy at The Trading Post still haunted her. *I should tell Deidre. But Alex didn't tell me anything for sure.*

Even the gossip around town had dwindled. Of course, there'd always be talk about the killings. She knew that years from now, people would still discuss every real and imagined detail. After all, the cases were a lot juicier than talking about cattle and corn prices.

Suddenly, she remembered her last thought before she fell asleep the night before. She jumped out of bed, brushed her teeth and put on a clean pair of jeans and her best top. She scribbled a quick note to Mom and rushed out the door.

A short time later, she peered through one of the cloudy side lite windows by the front door of The Trading Post. A long line extended past the checkout counter and towards the back of the store. Sam didn't even look up when she pushed through the entrance. She noticed he had that same resigned-to-my-fate look that he'd shown when she bought Toni's toy. She walked to the back of the line and continued to watch him. *He doesn't look like a murderer. But what does a murderer look like? He is weird looking though — his eyes are close set and there's too much space between his nose and mouth. He kinda resembles an ape.* In that instant, he glanced up at her and she felt her cheeks grow hot. She broke their gaze by looking down at her feet. For the first time, she noticed the weathered boards in the floor. If there'd ever been a finish on them, it was long gone. They were nearly white and full of deep grooves. She looked around. Dust motes floated in the sun's rays coming in the store-front windows where tiny cob webs nested in the corners. *Doesn't look like he cares about the place.*

Finally, when her turn in line came, she blurted, "I'm looking for a part-time job." *Real smooth, girl. Didn't even introduce yourself.*

Seemingly unaware of her discomfort, he turned and pulled some papers from a tray behind him and shoved them at her. "Fill out this application. Wait a minute — how old are you?"

"Um, sixteen." *Well, almost sixteen.*

"Guess I could use some help," he said, slapping a pen down on the counter.

She stepped to the side to let customers ahead of her while she worked on the form, making sure she got her birth date to reflect that she was indeed sixteen.

"'Bout finished there?"

She looked up to see the wave of people had vanished. "Yeah." She handed him the application, willing her hand not to tremble.

"How come you want a job?"

"Saving up for a cell phone." She looked him in the eye and tried to ignore her churning stomach.

"You know the expensive part is the monthly contract, right?"

"Sure," she said.

He shrugged and asked a few more questions, like what her grade point was, and if she had after-school activities. "Okay, you start tomorrow at eleven — too busy to train you today. Pay is $8.50 an hour. Don't be late — ever. Had plenty of kids who didn't have a clue about being on time."

"Don't worry. I'm very reliable." She breathed a sigh of relief and hurried out the door. *Can't believe how easy that was. I expected a lot more questions, like where I've worked before and stuff like that. Maybe it's a good thing he's having a busy morning. Now — to convince Mom.*

The next morning, Kendra wheeled her bike through the unlocked back door and into the storage area where Sam had told her to stow it. Her heart pounded. And not just from the ride. Even if she hadn't planned to secretly check up on Sam, she would've been nervous about her first job. But this was over the top. *Maybe I've signed on with a murderer.* The room began to spin and she leaned against the wall beside her bike. *Breathe girl, breathe.*

At that instant, Sam appeared in the doorway. "What's wrong?"

"Was afraid I'd be late. I rode too fast."

"Huh."

He doesn't look convinced. Great. He's already suspicious.
She started toward the interior of the store, her knees wob-
bling beneath her. "I'm fine. Really. So, what's first?"

At her question, he seemed to change gears. "Got some new
stock in. You can help put it out. And — this is important —
I want you to listen to how I deal with customers. They're
always right — no matter how annoying. Remember that."

She nodded and followed him to a cart piled high with
Western shirts.

He picked up a pricing gun and one of the shirts. "Did
you talk to your mom about your hours?"

Pushing her fear aside, she answered, "Yeah, she says I can
work one day on the weekend, and no more than two after-
noons during the week. And she wants me to finish in time to
be home before dark."

"That's reasonable."

"I usually watch my little sister during the summer so that
means Mom will have to pay daycare on the days I work."

"Sounds like your mom's cool." He showed her a price list
and how to mark the shirts correctly.

"Yeah. She knows how much I want that iPhone." She felt
her heart rate descending. *Maybe I imagined his doubtful look
when I arrived.*

"Time's up. I need you to fill out this tax form before you
leave," Sam said.

She looked at the dusty clock on the wall. She was amazed
at how quickly the day had gone. As promised, he'd shown
her how to mark and arrange new inventory for sale. Then

he'd taught her how to rearrange products that customers had handled and left out of place. Throughout the day, he'd call out to her to join him in conversations with customers.

"This is Kendra. She's learning the ropes," he'd say.

She was glad that he introduced her, but didn't put her on the spot to actually help anyone yet. Maybe she was wrong about this guy. He seemed nice enough.

The tax form he handed her looked like a foreign language. "Okay to take this home and bring it back on Tuesday?"

"Sure. And bring your social security card with you," he replied. "I need to make a copy."

Chapter 34

It wasn't long before Kendra mastered helping customers, stocking inventory, and even running the register. She admitted to herself she was freaking proud of her new skills. Between the new job and babysitting her sister, the summer days melted away.

Sometimes, she'd do something fun with Audrey and Lucas. When the weather threatened over 90 degrees, Lucas would drive them to the public swimming pool in Grand Island. Amazingly, Mr. and Mrs. Worth had accepted Lucas into their family. They allowed him to date their daughter, and even drive her places. She had to keep an eye on Toni, but that wasn't a problem; she loved the water and spent her entire time happily splashing around in the wading pool. The only hard part was convincing the little mermaid to climb out when it was time to leave.

Today was one of those scorchers, so they loaded suits, towels, suntan lotion, and Toni's swim toys in the car, and headed for some relief from the humid heat. When they arrived, Toni hurried to play with her friends in the kiddie pool. It was so crowded in the big pool that there was little room to actually swim. Most of the people were standing in the water to cool down. Audrey and Lucas arranged two of the deck chairs as close as possible to each other. Lucas draped one of his long, pale legs over Audrey's.

She couldn't help but notice how her friend filled out her turquoise bikini top. She glanced down at her own polka-dot suit. Nothing. When she'd turned fifteen, she'd wondered aloud to her mom if she'd ever need a bra. Mom had told her not to worry. "You've got plenty of time to deal with all that. Believe me, it's not all it's cracked up to be."

"What do you mean?" she'd asked.

"Sure, the guys like it, but mammograms aren't a walk in the park, and big-bosomed women have to deal with back pain. Plus, finding a bra that fits right can be a real challenge."

Well, I'd like to find out for myself.

Lucas interrupted her thoughts. "Hey — there's Johnny."

It was him all right. His ripped abs and toned arms brought a gasp to her lips. Then her heart sank. He was holding hands with someone. She felt Lucas and Audrey staring at her. "That's Shania Webb. Guess the rumors are true." *She's beautiful. One of those long-legged, straight-haired blondes I can't hold a candle to.* As the couple slowly made their way to the deep end of the pool, she stared at them through eyes that had suddenly gone blurry. "Please don't let him know we're here," she said. "Let's go!"

"We just got here," Lucas complained. "You guys broke up — you're gonna see him around. You gotta get used to it."

She started grabbing her things and stuffing them in her bag. "You don't get it — Audrey, you understand, don't you?"

Her friend nodded. "Yeah. Lucas, go get Toni."

At the mention of her sister's name, Kendra realized she'd forgotten about her. She usually checked on her every few seconds. *How long had it been?* She scrubbed the tears from her eyes and searched for Toni's pink suit with the yellow butterflies in the wading pool. "I don't see her!" She jumped up and ran to the group of little kids with Lucas and Audrey at her heels. No Toni. She didn't recognize the sound of her own voice as she cried out to her friends to go the opposite direction from her around the adult pool. She was vaguely aware of the hot concrete burning her bare feet as she ran along the pool's edge. When she met up with Audrey and Lucas, she knew they'd been around the whole perimeter. She fought back the panic that threatened to envelop her. "Audrey, go check the locker room! Lucas and I'll go 'round again."

Lucas said, "Gonna tell the lifeguard first."

Why didn't I think of that? She started out again, forcing herself to go slower this time, choking back the hysteria just beneath the surface. *I'm no use to Toni if I totally lose it.* The sunlight reflecting off the water blinded her. The tinny resonance of the lifeguard's megaphone calling for swimmers to clear the pool was muffled. People were using ladders or hoisting themselves onto the side of the pool to leave the water. A hush fell over the crowd. She looked up to see one of the lifeguards walk out onto the high dive and peer down into the water.

Audrey appeared at her side. "She's not in the locker room." Kendra had never seen such desperation in her friend's green eyes.

Then she heard a splash. She turned toward the four-foot section where there was no mistaking Lucas's redhead. She gaped around the stragglers still leaving the pool and saw him bend and lift her sister out of the water. Toni's limp arms flopped over Lucas's strong ones, as he carried her to the side of the pool where he gently laid her on the cement.

A nearby lifeguard spotted them and scaled down the side of his ladder as she ran toward the scene. She pushed through the gathering crowd to see him intent on CPR.

"Get back!" Lucas held his arms out wide and pushed at the gawkers. "Give him room to work."

She wanted to pray, but couldn't form words. She wanted to hold Audrey's hand, but couldn't reach out. After what seemed forever, she saw a trickle of water escape Toni's mouth. Did her sister's chest move? The silence was broken by sputters. More water drained from her pale lips and she began to cough. Soon, she started to cry. The lifeguard sat back on his haunches and looked relieved. People began talking excitedly. *Oh, my God! Is she really okay?*

The wide-eyed boy who had saved Toni's life said, "Come on. Let's go inside. My boss is there." He scooped her sister up like she was a sack of potatoes and carried her away. She ran after him, with her friends close behind.

A woman rushed forward and instructed the young man to put Toni on a cot in her office. "What happened?" As the lifeguard gave her his version of events, Kendra knelt down and took Toni's small hand in both of hers. As soon as she got the guard's story, she told him he could fill out his paperwork later and sent him back to pool duty. Then she addressed Lucas. "So, you pulled her from the pool?"

"Yeah."

"You her brother?"

Lucas shook his head.

"I'm her sister, and these are my friends," Kendra said. "Oh, Toni! What happened? You know you're s'posed to stay in the kiddie pool."

"My frien' threw my ball to me, but it went out. When I tried to get it, a big kid pushed me in the deep." Toni burst into tears again and clamped her chubby arms around Kendra for comfort.

"She was on the bottom of the pool and there were people standing right next to her, but they didn't even see her!" Lucas exclaimed. Drops of water flew as he shook his head from side to side in disbelief. "And the lifeguards didn't spot her, either!"

She shuddered at the thought of how close she'd come to losing her sister. "Thank you, Lucas. I owe you big time."

"That's why we tell those in charge of the little ones to watch 'em every minute. We'll have to fill out an incident report," the woman said. I'm the pool supervisor. She pointed at a name tag on her tee shirt. She gave Kendra an accusing stare. "How old are you?"

"Fifteen."

"Hmm. Where's your mom?"

"At work."

"It's obvious you're not ready for this responsibility."

Her cheeks burned. *She's right. I was so worried about Johnny and his new girlfriend that I forgot to check on the munchkin.*

The woman rose and went to a little refrigerator. She pulled out a juice box, and then rummaged in a drawer until she found a packet of crackers. As she handed them to Toni, she said, "You can sit up now, but you're to stay here for thirty minutes — to be sure you're okay. I'll tell you when you can go home, sweetheart." She patted the top of her blonde head.

The only sound on the drive home was the whir of the tires on the blacktop. Toni huddled against her in the back seat. She felt exhausted and could tell her sister was, too. *Poor kid. One minute she's safe and having fun, and the next, she's fighting for her life. And it's my fault.*

Finally, Lucas said, "I don't think we should go to the pool anymore."

Kendra knew what he meant — with Toni along. "Yeah, you're right." She hugged her sister closer.

That night, Mom took the news better than she'd expected. "It was an accident. Sounds like they had way too many people in the pool. And one of the lifeguards should've seen her. That's their job. Got half a notion to call 'em up and read 'em the riot act."

But that hadn't helped ease her guilty conscience. *If Mom had been there and seen the close call, she wouldn't be so cool about it. Maybe she's madder at me than she's letting on. Maybe doesn't want me to feel bad. But no matter what she says, I know I really screwed up.*

Another disturbing thought hit her. Alex Delgado — she'd nearly ended up like him — without a little sister. She couldn't imagine her life without Toni. It made her heart ache anew for him. *First losing his sister, and on top of that, his mom. It must be terrible.*

Chapter 35

In the weeks that followed, Kendra pushed any thoughts of Johnny and his new girlfriend from her mind. She kept busy looking after Toni, working at Sam Edelson's store, and of course, watching him for any weird behavior. It hadn't been too hard to forget about Johnny, but she knew when school started next week that would change. She dreaded seeing him in the hallway, with his arm looped around Shania.

Mrs. Snyderman's grating voice interrupted her thoughts. "I don't know about kids these days — all they want to do is talk and text on those fancy thinga-ma-jigs."

The gossipy housewife had been in the store with her brood of six for over an hour. It was past closing time and Kendra was fed up with keeping tabs on her kids while the rude woman bent Sam's ear. Overhearing her remark, she reached in her pocket and fingered her new iPhone. Knowing her work here had earned her this prized possession gave her a dot of pleasure in the midst of the little-kid madness. But she still wanted to call Audrey and shout, "This customer is keeping us here after closing and she's not even buying anything. Plus, her little brats are tearing the place apart." She remembered Sam's warning that the customer's always right, so instead, she mustered up the kindest voice she could, and said to one of the little boys removing the batteries from a remote-control race car, "You need to leave those in so people can see how it works."

"Don't have to mind you. You're not my mom!" the boy exclaimed, flinging the toy aside and running to the front of the store.

"What's the matter, Jerome?" Mrs. Snyderman asked.

"I wanna go home," the boy pouted.

"All right. Get your brothers and sisters." She gave him a little push.

Kendra sighed with relief and began straightening up after the little hurricanes. As she did, her eyes fell on the beading kits that were identical to the one she and Deidre had found on Glory's grave. Up until now, she hadn't noticed anything suspicious about Sam, only that he seemed grumpy and down a lot of the time. *He puts on a happy face for the customers, but when it's just us in the store, he's very different. But that doesn't make him a killer.* She picked up one of the beading kits and turned it over in her hands. She'd noticed them before and thought that made him the culprit. But the more she'd mulled it over, she knew that wasn't necessarily true. A customer could have bought it. *There's got to be a way to find out if it was him.* She heard something hit the floor in the next aisle and the patter of small feet. She headed there hoping it wasn't going to be too big of a cleanup. All the while, she kept thinking about the problem. Then something flashed in her brain. *That's it! I can set a trap for him!*

As soon as the annoying woman and her tribe left the store, she heard Sam locking up. "Could you help me with these toys? They made a real mess back here," she called.

"Yeah, I'll be there in a few minutes. I'm gonna close out the register first. You keep at it."

When she heard the sound of the creaking floor boards growing louder, she hurried to the craft section and pretended to be putting items in order.

"Almost done?" Sam asked.

"Yeah. It went faster than I thought." As he rounded the corner of the aisle, she held up one of the beading kits. "I think my little sister would like this." She watched him closely. He stopped mid-step and put his hand at his stomach. His eyes widened and a strange look flickered over his face. It was surprise, but something else, too — guilt.

Then just as rapidly as it had appeared, the look was gone, and he said, "I'll bet she would. You can have it. You earned it, chasing those darned kids around."

He did it. Murdered Glory. Her hands began to shake as she realized she'd been working alongside a killer and was now utterly alone with him. "Thanks, Toni will love it," she muttered.

He looked around the area. "You got everything back in order?"

She was suddenly painfully aware of how big he was. She looked at his bulging biceps and imagined his strong hands around her neck. "Yeah, all done. Well, better get going. My friend's meeting me at Mickey D's," she lied. She hurried toward the back to retrieve her bike, hoping he hadn't picked up on her fear.

It took every ounce of courage she had to keep from breaking into a dead run. The high ceilings and dingy walls seemed to be closing in on her. She heard the sound of his footsteps rushing after her. *He knows I know! I'm going to die in this mausoleum!* She began to sprint, but the toe of her shoe caught on one of the uneven floor boards and she sprawled forward. A scream caught in her throat.

"Wait! You forgot the toy for your sister." Then he caught up to her lying in the narrow aisle. "What happened? You trip?"

She cringed at his touch as he hauled her to her feet.

"Looks like you skinned up your knee pretty good. We better put something on it."

She stammered that she'd do it later, and took the beading kit from his meaty paw. Again, a strange look passed over his face — not guilt this time — more like suspicion. *I've really screwed up now.* She pushed through the swinging door into the back room, grabbed her bike and burst through the exit. When she was well out of sight of the store, she jumped from her bike and leaned it against the side of Pearl's Boutique. The shaking in her hands had now spread through her whole body. She hugged herself and slid down the rough brick wall to the ground. *Now what am I gonna do? I can never go back there. Gotta tell Deidre — but will she believe me? He didn't really say or do anything wrong.*

She sat like that a few minutes until she knew she had to face the inevitable. Still not steady enough to ride, she rose and walked her bike toward the police station. When she asked to see Deidre, the officer at the reception desk told her the chief always left at 5 o'clock on Saturdays.

"How 'bout Officer Prescott?"

"Might be out on patrol. I'll check," he said. "You're helping on the murder cases, aren't you?"

She nodded.

A few moments later, the man returned. "He's here, looking at some files. Said to go on back."

"What happened?" Chucky asked when he saw her. "You look like you saw a ghost."

She sank into a chair by his desk. "Wanted to talk to the chief, but I guess she's gone home."

He walked to the water cooler and brought a filled paper cup to her. "You can tell me what's going on, especially if it's about Glory Delgado or Robert O'Connor. I'm second in command on the cases." He puffed out his chest.

"Thought you weren't looking into them anymore."

"Well, that's not exactly true — we wanted people to think that — maybe give us an edge. 'Specially since the chief's idea of flushing out the killer at the town meeting didn't pan out."

"Yeah, I remember her telling the town there were fingerprints on the kit at Glory's grave, even though, we all knew there weren't." She took a gulp of the water. "Well — news flash. I know who killed her. And it has to do with that toy."

Chucky's Adam's apple bobbed up and down. "What?"

She launched into what Alex had told her about Sam visiting the Delgado farm on a pretty regular basis. "So, I got a job at The Trading Post to keep tabs on him."

"Does the chief know?" His eyes bulged.

"Umm. No. Didn't figure she'd be too keen on it."

"Got that right." He arched his eyebrows at her. "So, what happened?"

"Just so you know, the chief never told me he was a suspect so I felt safe working with him — 'til tonight." She laid out the whole scene, emphasizing how Edelson had stopped in his tracks when she held up the beading kit. "I didn't know a look could say so much. The chief was dead-on about body language."

"Never did like that guy. I'll call Deidre as soon as we get you in a car and on your way home. Stay there 'til you hear from her. I know she'll wanna hear the details directly from you."

"But I've got my bike," she protested.

"No problem. The officer will be sure it gets safe passage, too." He smiled reassuringly at her.

Chucky was right. The phone was ringing when she was barely in the door. The chief listened without interruption while Kendra repeated the scenario at the store.

"Be at the station first thing tomorrow." She could tell by Deidre's frosty tone that she was in major trouble.

The next morning, she sat in front of the chief's desk and braced herself for the storm ahead.

"I don't know who I'm madder at — you or me. I should've known you'd be up to no good."

"Sorry." She pulled at a loose string on her shirt cuff.

"Did you know Chucky was suspicious of him early on, and I even interviewed him at his home?"

"No kidding?"

"We thought he was a little peculiar, but couldn't pinpoint anything specific. So lately he's been off our radar. Tell me again what happened last night. Don't leave out a single thing."

She went through the whole scene, trying to remember every word and action. As she'd feared, Deidre said it was all circumstantial.

"I know, but if you could've seen the look on his face. He killed Glory. Without a doubt."

"I'm afraid there's plenty of doubt. We need something a lot more concrete than just your opinion. And what about O'Connor? I'm sure they were both murdered by the same person. I could buy Edelson maybe — just maybe — killing Glory — because we've connected him to her — but why would he off O'Connor, too?" Deidre scratched her head. "You told your mom about this?"

"Yeah, she freaked out. Said I had to quit immediately. Like I hadn't already decided that." She rolled her eyes.

"Good. You shouldn't be anywhere near that guy. Now get outta here, and for once in your puny little life, mind your own business."

She was almost out the door when the chief called, "Hey, wait a sec. Ever notice if he wore cologne?"

"Yeah. Would knock me over first thing in the morning."

Deidre's voice rose an octave. "Could you tell what it was?"

"Men's fufu is a way outta my know-how. Why?"

"Nothing important. Just watch your back, young lady."

Her response didn't fool her for a minute. Obviously, the cologne played into the case. *Seems like she could tell me — after all, she did make me a police cadet.*

The next day, after she'd finished patching up her damaged ego from Deidre's reprimands, she summoned the courage to call Edelson. She told him her mom didn't want her working during the school year.

"School doesn't start for another week."

"Mom says I need time to shop for school clothes and stuff." She swallowed. "Sorry to do this out of the blue. Didn't know she was gonna make me quit."

"You know you're being extremely inconsiderate, don't you? I count on you being here. The least you could do is give two weeks' notice." She could hear the anger over the line.

She wanted to point out that he'd been doing fine by himself before she applied for the job, but she only repeated, "I'm so sorry, Sam. Really."

He clicked off without so much as a goodbye. She let out a huge sigh. The realization that she'd been working with a murderer had brought back the terrifying nightmares just when they were finally dissipating. She'd never forget how that monster, Grimsby, had kidnapped her and taken her over two state lines before he was caught. She still thanked the universe that perfect strangers had picked up on her signals for help and reported their suspicions. She knew if it weren't for them, she wouldn't be alive.

So, the nightmares are back and on top of that, it looks like nothing will come of my account of Sam's reaction to the beading kit. She threw herself on the sofa and mentally danced around in a private pity party until she realized how pathetic she was. *You knew what you were getting into when you dove right into Glory's case. So, things aren't goin' your way. Big deal. Don't be such a baby.*

A few days passed and the sting of the chief's rebuke and the realization that nothing would come from her sacrifice of working with a killer faded. She began to think about starting high school. It was a big deal — but unlike working undercover, she was facing the same worries her classmates were — will the older kids like me? — will the lessons be too hard? — will I be able to get to class on time? She and Audrey had been school shopping — not that her friend needed anything. Her closet was already bursting with the latest cool clothes. There was a time when she'd been jealous of Audrey, but it didn't bother her anymore. And if her friend was appalled by the fact that Kendra's wardrobe was from Wal-Mart and sometimes even Goodwill, she never let it show.

When they'd discussed her anxiety about seeing Johnny with Shania when school began, Audrey said, "You're way better than her. They won't last through the first semester. Johnny likes girls with brains. She may be pretty, but she's not the sharpest blade on the rototiller."

"I don't know why I even care," Kendra said. "Sometimes he made me feel smothered — now I can do whatever I want."

"Come on girl, admit it, you know you've got it major bad for him."

She smiled a little. "Yeah, guess you're right."

When her first day as a freshman began, and she glimpsed Johnny and Shania walking to class, it wasn't as devastating as she'd expected. Sure, it tugged at her heart when she saw him bend to whisper something in her ear, but she remembered Audrey's words about Johnny liking smart girls, and held her head high.

But her stab at just being a normal teenager vanished when Deidre called her a few days later. "We've been watching Edelson, and he's not doing anything to betray himself. Got an idea for figuring out if this is our guy. But it involves you and your mom. Could you both come down to the station?"

"You're kidding, right? You said what I reported wasn't any help and to mind my own business."

"Wouldn't ask if we had any other options."

She wanted to tell the chief to take a flying leap, but the part of her that couldn't wait to hear the plan refused to be silenced. She clicked off and called her mom at work — something she never did. But after all, this was an emergency.

"I'm not crazy about this, but okay — we'll see what she wants. She is the top cop after all — can't just ignore her." Teresa sighed. "I'll call the day care and tell them we'll be a little late picking up Toni. Meet me at the police station at 5 o'clock."

Kendra had to admit Deidre was very persuasive when she wanted to be. First, she served them homemade peanut butter cookies from Sadie's Café and chatted pleasantly for a few minutes. Then she impressed on her mom how much she and the Finchville Police Department appreciated all they'd done to help in the past.

Finally, she said, "So, here's the thing. We have matching unknown DNA from both crime-scenes. We ran the samples through CODIS, but nothing popped. So, our killer isn't in the system. We suspect Sam Edelson might be our guy, even though our suspicions are based more on gut feel than fact. We don't have enough for or an arrest, or even a warrant. If we could get his DNA, we'd run it against the unknown samples and if it's a match, we can bring him in." She stopped talking and looked steadily at Teresa. "I've got a plan to do this, but it involves you and your daughter, Mrs. Morgan."

Kendra was dumbstruck when she heard Deidre's idea.

Chapter 36

Kendra could hardly believe they were doing this. As she and her mom dressed, she asked, "Do you think you can pull this off?" Would she be able to carry off the charade? She'd been working with Sam all summer and deceiving him about why she was there, but this was all new to Mom. On the other hand, she had to admit she was worried about facing Sam after she'd quit so abruptly. *He won't be happy to see me; that's for sure. And, if he is the killer, we could be setting ourselves up for disaster.*

Teresa swallowed nervously. "Yeah, I think so."

Her response didn't reassure her, but there was no going back now. The plan was locked in.

A short while later, Deidre picked them up and gave them a ride to within a couple blocks of The Trading Post. She reminded Kendra to call immediately if Sam did anything threatening. "You won't have to say a word. I'll know it's you by your caller identification. Chucky's in his patrol car on State Street, too — so we can both be there right away."

It was just a little before opening time. She knew Sam's habit was to have a smoke behind the store before he started his day. The chief had told them that what they were doing was perfectly legal. "Remember, it's important to get a fresh sample in order to prove chain of evidence. You've got to see him toss the cigarette."

Sure enough, as she and Mom rounded the corner of the building and started down the littered alleyway, she spotted him leaning against the building wall and puffing away on his menthol. Suddenly, a cold fear stopped her in her tracks. She wished the wind tumbling the bits of trash around them would tumble her away, too. *He could grab the bat he keeps in the back room for protection from burglars and bludgeon us both in a matter of seconds.*

Teresa reached out and grabbed her. "What're you doing? Come on!"

And I was worried about Mom holding it together.

"You're out early," he said as they approached. "This mom?"

It felt like she had a corn cob in her throat. She couldn't swallow, let alone speak. When she failed to answer, Teresa said, "Yes, that's me. Thought we'd come by and get my daughter's paycheck so we can finish up school shopping."

"Figured you'd be around eventually," Sam said grudgingly. "Come on in." He took a last drag on the smoke, dropped it, and used his boot to grind it out. Then he turned to unlock the door.

As her mom followed him into the darkened store, she took a deep breath to steady herself and grabbed two small plastic bags out of her hoodie pocket. Per Deidre's instructions, she used one bag as a shield over her hand and popped the butt into the other baggie. Specks of dirt and tiny rocks clung to it. *Can't do anything about that.* She jammed the bags back into her pocket and quickened her step to catch up with Mom and Sam.

At the checkout counter, he pulled an envelope from a drawer. "Here." He handed it to Kendra with a grim look on his face. She felt her right eyelid begin to twitch uncontrollably.

"Something wrong?" He stared at her.

She was still tongue-tied.

Teresa jumped in again. "Thank you, Mr. Edelson. So good of you to give my daughter a summer job."

He only grunted in reply and narrowed his eyes at them.

"Well, come on, honey. Better get going." Teresa grabbed her sleeve. They broke into a dead run once they were clear of the store. "Did you get it?" her mom asked, her calm demeanor suddenly gone.

"Yes!"

"Are you all right?" Deidre asked when they jumped into the cruiser, gasping for air.

"Yeah, Kendra suddenly forgot how to talk, so I hope he didn't suspect anything," Teresa said. "That guy is creepy." She turned to Kendra. "I'm still not over the fact that you were working for him knowing he might be a killer!"

In the safety of the car, she found her voice, even if it was as quavery as the rest of her body. "Honestly, I didn't think he was. Only did it to make Alex feel better." She knew she wasn't being entirely truthful, but her mom's accusation put her on the defense. Once more, she repeated what she'd already told her and Deidre several times. "Alex told me Sam had been out to their place a lot to drop off stuff Glory ordered. I never felt afraid 'til that night I showed him the jewelry kit and he gave me that weird look. Right away, I went to you and the cops."

The chief hurried to calm the situation. "Hey, thanks for going the extra mile. Most folks wouldn't stick their necks out like you two did. Sure do appreciate it! I'll drop you at home and then I'll drive this to Grand Island for testing." She held up the evidence bag Kendra had handed her. "I'll ask for a rush on it — it'll still take a while — but I'll definitely let you know when we get the results."

She gave Kendra a look. "In the meantime, you're to suspend all of your sleuthing activities, understood? Cadets never, ever, work on their own."

"No problem," she gulped. And this time, she really meant it.

"Good," Deidre said. "And not a word of this to Alex, or anyone else."

Chapter 37

Kendra threw herself into Finchville High School's scene. She loved it. The kids were more grown up than at Spencer Middle. Some of them, anyway. And the teachers were definitely cooler. They didn't treat their students like first graders. Mr. Brown, her English teacher, summed it up. "You may think freshman year isn't a big deal — that your grades don't matter. Think again. If you're considering college, you need to shoot for a "B" or better grade point average." He looked over his horn-rimmed glasses. "And we're not here to babysit you. It's totally up to you."

As he passed out a synopsis for the quarter — and explained what in the heck a "synopsis" was — she knew she was ready for the challenge. "I'm not going to remind you every day what we're working on, or when assignments are due. Refer to this paper. It's all laid out for you."

She was glad school gave her something to concentrate on while they waited for the DNA results from the crime lab. *Those lab nerds take forever.* At the back of her mind, she worried about Edelson. *Is he suspicious of me? If he is, he wouldn't be stupid enough to try anything, would he? That would only point to his guilt.*

It took her a couple of days to realize that a black-and-white followed her at a distance throughout the day: to and from Toni's daycare, to and from school, to and from wherever she went. *Does Deidre really think I'd do something idiotic? Well, she doesn't have to worry about me poking around. Now that I'm sure Sam's the killer, I'm not going anywhere near the guy.*

Two more days passed and she was fed up with being followed everywhere. She was riding her bike to Audrey's when she caught a glimpse of the patrol car. It was stopped at a red light. She flipped her bike around and raced back to it before the light changed. She peered through the tinted window. No surprise. It was Deidre. The window came down. "Why are you tracking me?" she sputtered.

Deidre motioned her to the curb as she pulled the cruiser over. "I think you know."

She leaned in the window. "Kids at school are noticing. They're quizzing me. I've been playing dumb, but they know something's up. And what if Edelson sees you tailing me?"

The chief pulled her unhappy face. "Okay, I'll ease up, but promise me you won't get clever."

"Scout's honor," she said, raising her hand in the Girl Scout salute. "Honestly, you gotta believe me. The guy totally freaks me out."

Deidre gave her a piercing stare. "All right, I believe you. But remember, not a word of this to anyone. And keep an eye out for him. Call me immediately if you see him hanging around.

"Don't have to tell me that." As she watched the cruiser drive away, she had to admit to herself she was bursting to tell Audrey that Edelson was a suspect. She'd fed her friend just enough detail to satisfy her, but had held back that they had their sights on Sam. She could hardly believe it herself — a respected member of the business community — a murderer! But she'd sworn she wouldn't breathe a word and she didn't like breaking promises. Thank goodness, she had Mom to talk to. Nearly every night after Toni was tucked into bed, they'd re-live the scary experience of going to pick up her paycheck. And for the umpteenth time, they'd wonder how long before the DNA results came back.

That very night, Deidre called to tell Mom that they'd informed Ricky Delgado they had a possible suspect in the case. Kendra was sure Mr. Delgado would've told Alex by now. *That must be giving them some hope. But I'm glad Alex is at Spencer Middle so I don't have to see him at school. I know I'd probably run my mouth. The DNA must've been Edelson's if they called Mr. Delgado.*

In the days that followed, tons of rumors flew around the school, triggered by the presence of the black-and-white which had been tailing her. But they were so far from the truth that she couldn't imagine what planet they originated from. Keeping her head down and her mouth shut was hard, but she did it. Kids she didn't even know came up to her and quizzed her. Yeah, the snoopiness of the town was alive and well. It was hard staying quiet, but she'd gotten good at playing dumb.

Then one day in late September the principal came to her sixth period class. She whispered something in the teacher's ear. The usual rustling in the room stopped. The teacher said, "Kendra, gather your things and go with Principal Harding."

All eyes turned to stare at her. She felt her face grow pink as she swept her book and papers into her backpack.

In the hallway, Chucky stood with thumbs hooked into his wide belt.

"Officer Prescott wants you to go with him on police business," the principal said. She had a little smile on her face, like she knew something good, but didn't want to say what.

"Um. Okay," was all she could manage. She threw her backpack over her shoulder and did her best to keep up with Chucky's long strides out of the building.

When he reached the outer doors, he stopped for her to catch up. "We've got Sam Edelson coming in for questioning. Chief says since you helped on the case, you can watch the interrogation."

She stopped in her tracks. "What?"

He ignored her and pushed through the doors.

She found her feet and hurried after him as he strode down the sidewalk toward the parking lot. The feeling that rushed through her was indescribable. *This must be joy. Real joy! Whatever it is, I don't want it to stop.* "Really?" she squealed. "She said that?" She piled into the car and threw her backpack down at her feet.

"Yup," he replied, as he backed out of the visitors' parking spot. "She called your mom, too. She can't get out of work, but told us it was okay for you to come on down. Personally,

I'm not so sure it's a good idea, but who am I to say." He shrugged his bony shoulders.

When they arrived at the station, Bianca told them Deidre was already in the interrogation room with Edelson. "Follow me," Chucky said. He stationed her behind a one-way mirror in a small, stuffy room, not much bigger than a closet. A trickle of sweat formed on the back of her neck. "You can watch from here. That's Marvin McElroy, head of the CSU unit." He gestured at a stranger looking through the mirror a couple of feet away.

The man gave her a nod and a quick hello as she stepped up beside him. When she spotted Sam Edelson facing the mirror with his meaty hands resting on a long table, she was too thunderstruck to reply to the man.

Deidre sat with her back to them, a tape recorder and a notepad at her fingertips. Chucky entered the room and leaned his lanky frame against the wall. From somewhere in his shirt pocket, he retrieved a toothpick and slid it between his lips. "Anything useful yet?" his voice came through a little box on the wall next to the one-way.

"We're just getting started — the recorder's on and he's been read his rights and we dispensed with time, place, etc.," the chief said. Her words were clipped. "Now Sam, we need to know what you were doing the day Glory Delgado was murdered."

The man glared. "How am I supposed to know? When was it?"

"April second, Wednesday," Deidre replied.

"I would've been at the store."

"All day? Don't you close for lunch?"

As he continued to stare hatefully at her, he admitted that he did. "A man's gotta eat, doesn't he?"

Chucky pulled up a chair next to Edelson. "Watch your attitude, mister."

"I'm not doing anything wrong." He turned to Chucky. Then, returning his gaze to Deidre, he asked in a more reasonable tone, "Why would I hurt Glory? She was one of my best customers. Everybody in town liked her, including me."

"How *much* did you like her?"

"What are you insinuating?"

"She wasn't a bad-looking woman," the chief said. "Maybe you developed a little crush? Or maybe more than a crush? People say there's no girlfriend in the picture."

He stiffened in his chair. "You're nuts. We were friends — that's it. The bottom feeders in this town have nothing better to do than gossip."

"Okay, let's say you weren't having an affair. But one side wanted to — your side. Maybe you had ways of trying to persuade her?"

The man seemed unmoved. Through the glass, Kendra saw no trace of humanity. It made her feel hollow inside. *Maybe he's a sociopath or a narcissist like Deidre suggested, but all I know is, he's scary!*

"All right, I can see you don't want to talk about that right now, so let's discuss Robert O'Connor," the chief continued.

"What about him?"

"The coroner puts his death on Thursday, April tenth. What were you doing that day?"

"Same thing as always. Pretty much spend all my time at the store."

"Time of death is in question. Could've been at night after you closed up." She leaned forward a little.

Kendra drew a breath. The fact that O'Connor may've been killed at night was news to her. She could imagine the hard look Deidre was giving Sam. *Been on the receiving end of that.*

"Didn't know the guy. Far as I know, he never even came into the store."

"Don't you have a life outside of work? Maybe you ran into him at Sadie's Café, or at one of our taverns?" Deidre's voice now sounded laid back, like they were discussing something as ordinary as the latest showing of a sitcom. She leaned back in her chair.

The man shook his head. "I'm beat by the time I get home. I fix my dinner and do the books. By that time, I'm ready to hit the sack."

"Speaking of that, we'll be taking a look at those."

"What? Why do you need to see my accounts?" He looked startled.

"Standard procedure."

"Hold up! You can't haul me down here like this! And now you want to look at my financials? I'm outta here." He pushed back from the table and started to rise.

Chucky stumbled a little on the table leg as he rushed over to the suspect. He grabbed him by the shirt and settled him roughly back in the chair. "Listen up. We've been real polite up to now. No more. You're gonna get straight with us. And now." He bit down hard on the toothpick.

She couldn't help but smile at Chucky's awkwardness. But she had to admit she was impressed with his take-charge attitude. She'd never seen that side of him. The chief rose and moved away from the table. *I know what this is. They're playing good cop, bad cop. I've seen this on TV true crime shows.*

He went nose-to nose with the suspect and repeated the same questions Deidre had asked, over and over, ramping up the intensity each time. She watched breathlessly as their subject became increasingly frustrated. The door of the observation room opened, bringing her back to where she stood. Bianca poked her head in. "How's it going?"

"So far, he's sticking to his story — he doesn't know a thing," she whispered.

"Don't worry, they can't hear us. Looks like it's going to be a while," Mr. McElroy said.

She turned to him in surprise. She'd been so intent on the interrogation that she'd forgotten the man standing within feet of her.

Bianca dragged a tall stool over to the window. "You'd better sit. He's right. They're just getting started — unless Edelson asks for an attorney, it's gonna be a while."

"Why doesn't he?" Kendra asked.

"A lot of these guys think they're smarter than the cops. Or that if they ask for a lawyer, they'll look guilty. It's rad stuff though, isn't it?" Bianca blew a huge bubble with her wad of bubble gum and hurried out.

Kendra nodded and turned her attention back to the window to see Deidre grabbing a seat at the table. This time she sat at the other end. *Much better. I can see her facial expressions.* She remembered Deidre asking her about Sam's cologne. *I wonder if she's checking for any trace of it.*

The chief gave Chucky an almost imperceptible nod. She said, "Sam, you might be interested to know we've got a search warrant for your home and business. It's being carried out now."

He stared at her in disbelief. "You can't do that! I'll sue!"

"We can, and we are," Deidre said quietly. "You'd be smart to start with the truth this minute, while it can still help you."

"That's ridiculous! I want an attorney." He looked around the airless room as though he hoped one would materialize from the gray walls.

Ah, there it is. He knows he's in trouble now. Kendra was spellbound.

"Okay. Chucky will ask Bianca to call one. Who's your lawyer?"

"Hell, I don't have one! Never needed one." He rubbed his hands over his stomach.

"Jan Emineth practices criminal law in Grand Island. As far as I know, we don't have any lawyers who defend murderers here in Finchville," Deidre said drily.

"Call her!" he demanded.

"Please?"

"Goddammit! Please!"

"You heard the man." Deidre nodded to Chucky, who sauntered out of the room like he had all day.

At the lull in the questioning, she became aware of her own surroundings. She felt like the small room was closing in on her. She couldn't imagine how hemmed in Edelson must feel. The interrogation room wasn't much bigger than the one she and the CSU guy were in. And it was completely bare, except for the table and three chairs. There wasn't even a clock on the wall. She glanced at her own watch — six o'clock. *Four hours had passed!* Deidre's voice interrupted her thoughts.

"Sam, while we wait for your attorney, you might like to know we have evidence that links you to both murders. You're not helping yourself by holding out on us." She shifted her wide bulk on the chair.

"What? What evidence?" His eyes grew wide.

"We've got DNA that links you to both crime-scenes."

"That's my cue," the man standing beside her said. She watched him hustle into the interrogation room with Chucky close behind him. He pulled a fat, zippered notebook from under his arm and began laying out an array of papers on the table.

"This is Marvin McElroy. He heads up the state's CSU. He'll explain in more detail," Deidre said. "But I must caution you, since you've asked for an attorney, we can't interrogate you. However, we can share with you what we know. That's why Mr. McElroy's here."

The man didn't even acknowledge the suspect. Instead, he simply and methodically presented the DNA evidence the state had collected.

As he took in the reports, Edelson's front began to crumble. "When's my lawyer getting here?" He ran his hands through his hair.

Chucky shifted from his position on the wall. "Oh, forgot to mention, when I called, the voice message said her office was closed. I left a message on her cell, though."

Edelson clenched his fists. Then he rolled his eyes to the ceiling. "I don't get it. How'd you get my DNA?"

Even through the glass she saw droplets of sweat pop on his forehead. She almost felt sorry for him.

"The newest addition to our team helped with that," Deidre said. "You'll hear all about that at trial. I'm thinking Glory was pretty rude to you, even though you bent over backwards for her. Some women are unappreciative that way," she said sympathetically. "I'm sure you didn't mean for anything bad to happen."

Her moment of compassion for the suspect was replaced with an icy fear when she heard the words, "the newest addition to their team." *Oh no! She's talking about Mom and me!*

Chapter 38

Deidre's statement that they had Edelson's DNA — and that a new addition to the task force had collected it — had sent both Edelson and Kendra into a panic. Now the suspect dripped sweat and Kendra hugged herself in terror. At that instant, her mom came in from work. Seeing her daughter's stricken face, Teresa rushed over to her. "What's wrong?"

"Deidre just told Sam that someone new to their team collected his DNA."

"You're kidding! Did she give our names?"

"No."

"Didn't think she would," Teresa said.

"But what if he finds out it was us?"

"Good question. I can't see her putting either of us in danger though. She must know what she's doing — I hope!" They turned back to the window to see the suspect slumped forward. His feet tapped the floor furiously.

She quickly told her mom what had happened so far, then asked, "Where's Toni?"

"I called Peg. She came right over and said she'd give her dinner and tuck her into bed." Teresa reached into her bag, pulled out a bottle of cold water and handed it to her.

"Thanks, Mom. So hot in here." She rolled the bottle over her feverish forehead.

They were amazed to hear Edelson say, "Okay, I'll tell you what happened."

"But you asked for a lawyer. To continue, you'll have to waive that right," Deidre said.

"Yeah, I do," he muttered.

"A little louder for the recorder, Sam."

"I waive my damned rights!" he shouted.

"Calm down." The chief waited for him to collect himself. "So, were you and Glory having an affair?"

"No — I told you that before. Not that I didn't want to," he mumbled. "But I wasn't good enough."

"Oh?"

Minutes passed. She saw Deidre and Chucky exchange glances. "Chucky, why don't you go get us a soda?"

After he left, Sam took a deep breath. "I drove out there to deliver another one of those frilly dresses I'd ordered from an Omaha store for her. She could never get enough of the little girls' clothes — you know how messed up she was about that. Chrissakes, the whole town knew. When I got there, she told me she didn't have the money for it." He began rocking back and forth.

Kendra saw the agony in his face. It wasn't what she expected. *Where's the ruthless killer?*

He continued swaying as he clutched his middle. "That was nothing new — told her no problem — I'd put it on her credit card. But she said Ricky had thrown a fit about all the charges and I'd have to send it back. I told her I couldn't, the manager at the store was doing me a big favor. And you know what she did?"

Deidre shook her head.

"She didn't even answer me. Just walked back into that hellhole of a kitchen. That's when the wall of red washed over me."

"Wall of red?"

"Yeah, sometimes when I get mad, it's like a red ooze takes over and I can't see or hear right. She was dismissing me, like I was nothing. A big fat zero. All my life women have looked down their noses at me. I know I'm not much to look at, but I'm a successful businessman — I could take good care of 'em. I thought she was different."

Even though his voice was low, Kendra heard the rage gathering in it.

"I told myself to calm down. I said, 'Glory, aren't you even gonna ask me in for an iced tea?' She said no, she had to get dinner for Ricky. She'd cook for *him* and I didn't even rate a cold drink." He was visibly trembling now.

At that moment, Chucky returned with the sodas and passed them around. "That must've been tough." Deidre leaned over and whispered something to her officer.

The chief's probably telling Chucky to keep quiet since he's finally talking.

Edelson popped the top on the can and took a long drink of his soda. "Yeah, it was tough all right. You got any idea what I sacrificed for that woman?" He paused a moment. "I made my way through the crap on the back porch and followed her into the kitchen. She told me I couldn't stay — after all I'd done for her. Something gave way in me." He got a faraway look, as if remembering. "I think I tried to kiss her. She wiped her mouth like I was dirt and yanked away from me. She tried to step over a pile of junk and lost her footing. Her head hit the corner of the table, but she jumped up and kept going. She was actually trying to run away from me. Ha — what a joke. There was no running through that trash heap. As she went through the house, boxes teetered and fell. Once a lamp came crashing down that was on top of a humongous stack of newspapers, barely missing her. I caught up to her in the hallway before she reached the front door."

"And then what?"

He gulped like a fish at the stale air in the room. "She was yelling hysterically. Couldn't even tell what she was saying. Just knew I had to stop her. I picked up the closest thing and hit her. Just once." He covered his eyes with his thick hands. "I didn't mean to hurt her. Honest to God. But I panicked. I knew Ricky would be in soon, so I got out of there — she was alive when I left."

"What did you hit her with?"

"Some kinda paperweight."

"So, you left her there — alone and bleeding?" Deidre gave him a scathing look.

He nodded. "Yeah, I took the paperweight and got out of there. I'm sorry. I'm so, so sorry!"

"What did you do with it?"

"Tossed it in a ditch on the way back to town."

"Hmm. Seems like for someone who couldn't hear or see good 'cuz of 'the red ooze,' you recall things quite clearly."

"Well, that's the way I remember it anyway. Might not've happened like that at all."

"If you were so sorry about hurting Glory, seems like you would've called for help, and you sure wouldn't have disposed of the weapon. And tell me — are you that sorry about Robert O'Connor, too? Remember, we've got your DNA at both crime-scenes."

Mother and daughter stiffened at the mention of the DNA again.

"How'd you say you got my DNA?"

"You'll find out soon enough. No need to worry about that now," Deidre replied. "I believe we were talking about O'Connor."

"*You* were talking about him. I'm not sayin' another friggin' thing 'til my lawyer gets here."

I can't believe he confessed. He must've wanted to get Glory's death off his chest — he was in love with her. Maybe leaving her to die finally got to him. She wanted to ask her mom what she thought, but didn't want to miss a word of the conversation.

Deidre looked at her watch. "Guess we've put in a day's work. We'll break until Ms. Emineth can be here tomorrow if I can hear one more thing from you."

"Yeah?"

"Did you play a part in O'Connor's murder? That's it — no details needed right now — just want to know if you were involved."

His eyebrows rose. "No way am I talkin' about that."

"Hmm. Okay, maybe we should stay a while longer. I didn't have any plans for tonight. Did you, Chucky?"

"Nope. I can always run out for burgers if we have to stay 'til midnight or so." He grinned.

Deidre rose from her chair and began circling the table. "Okay, let's start again, Sam. Tell us what you were doing on the day O'Connor died. Include everything from when you got up in the morning 'til you went to bed that night." She received only silence in return. She and Chucky took turns repeating the demand until it seemed to take on a life of its own.

At last he muttered, "I already told you. I was at The Trading Post all day and home all night."

"Can anyone confirm you were home all night?"

"For God's sake, you know I live alone!"

"How'd your DNA get in Robert O'Connor's barn?"

"I don't know, I don't know, I don't know! You can't do this to me! I told you, I'll sue your ass off!"

Kendra stared at her mom in disbelief, who returned the same shocked look. *Now we're seeing the real Edelson — the rage lurking there, just beneath the surface. Poor Glory. She probably had no idea what he was capable of.*

"Won't be the first time, Sam. But you know what? The judgments always seem to come down on the side of law enforcement. So, you do what you gotta do."

That night, Kendra's nerves were still jangling. She tried to calm herself by listening to her favorite tunes in her bedroom. She'd discussed the whole experience repeatedly with her mom and neither of them could believe what they'd witnessed. Losing the battle with her conscience, she waited for her mom to shower so her conversation wouldn't be overheard. She pulled out her iPhone and dialed Audrey.

"Hello," her friend mumbled.

"Audrey. You're not going to believe this."

"What?"

She launched into the explanation of how she and her mom had gotten Edelson's DNA.

"Why didn't you tell me sooner? What kinda best friend are you?"

Kendra explained how she and her mom had been sworn to secrecy.

That unruffled her BFF's feathers — she was a much bigger supporter of following orders than Kendra. "Start over, and don't leave out a thing."

So, she repeated the whole story about going to Deidre with her suspicion that Edelson had killed Glory — and how scared she'd been when she and Mom secretly collected the DNA sample. Then she launched into her account of the interrogation and the confession, with Audrey chiming in at intervals to express her amazement. "And guess what? I get to go back tomorrow, too. And his attorney's going to be there."

"OMG, Kendra! You're so lucky!"

"Don't I know it?"

"You've got to call me as soon as you're outta there, okay? I can't wait to hear what happened."

"Don't worry, I will — but Audrey, YOU CANNOT BREATHE A WORD OF THIS TO ANYONE! I promised Deidre I wouldn't tell a soul about what's happening with the investigation. Even Ricky Delgado doesn't know what's going on yet, just that they have a suspect. Deidre said she wants to get all the facts first before she calls him. PROMISE ME!"

"Double pinky-swear. Not a word to anyone!"

Chapter 39

The next morning, Kendra and her mom once again sat in the airless room. Teresa had called her boss and asked for the evening shift. "I wouldn't have missed this for anything!" she'd exclaimed. They were perched side by side on their stools, noses nearly pressed against the one-way mirror in anticipation.

Chucky popped in to confirm the speaker was turned on for them. He showed them how to adjust the volume if they wanted to. "Almost ready to start."

A couple of minutes later, they watched in fascination, as he led the man who had struck terror in their hearts, into the interview room. She noticed he was walking funny. Her eyes fell to his feet — he was hobbled by leg cuffs. She stared, amazed, as Chucky sat him down and unlocked one end of the cuffs, only to reattach it to the table leg. She exchanged looks with Mom, who appeared equally surprised.

"Your lawyer will be in shortly," Chucky said. Soon he returned with bottled waters and a tall, elegant-looking woman. She placed her briefcase on the table and retrieved a thick stack of papers.

Chucky left the room while the killer and the woman representing him, huddled together and spoke in whispers.

"Oh, I wish they'd talk louder!" Kendra exclaimed, fiddling with the volume knob on the speaker.

"They may suspect there's someone on the other side of this mirror."

"But it'd be against the law for cops to listen in while he's talking to his lawyer, right?"

"Yeah, but attorneys are suspicious by nature. S'pose they have to be," Teresa conceded.

To Kendra, the secretive conversation seemed to go on forever, but finally the woman rose and painstakingly straightened her suit jacket. "I'll let them know we're ready." She disappeared for just a minute, then returned and sat beside her client, tapping her pen on the table.

The door opened, and Deidre and her officer entered. Chucky was carrying a video camera and tripod, which he set up directly in front of Edelson. Of course, he had his uniform on, but Kendra was surprised to see the chief in street clothes. She wore dark brown slacks with an apricot blouse and rust blazer. She thought the colors suited her olive complexion, but she wondered why she wasn't wearing her uniform. *Maybe she wants them to make no mistake about her power. Let them know this is her house and she can wear whatever she wants.*

"'Morning." Deidre motioned toward the camera. "As you can see, we'll have a video and audio record of the interview. Ready to begin?"

The attorney looked at her client and nodded.

The chief spoke in a monotone, almost as though she were reading a weather forecast. "This is Deidre Goodwin, head of the Finchville Police Department, Finchville, Nebraska.

Present are Charles Prescott, police officer, Jan Emineth, attorney, and Sam Edelson. Mr. Edelson was arrested yesterday for the murders of Glory Delgado and Robert O'Connor. He was read his Miranda rights at that time." She continued in the same manner, giving the date and time and a short summary of Edelson's confession to attacking Glory, and their intent to now question him about O'Connor's death.

The chief looked from Jan Emineth to Edelson. "Your attorney has been advised of all previous actions of the department and the evidence gathered against you. You've had time to discuss this together?"

"You know I have," Edelson grumbled.

"Just confirming for the record," Deidre said mildly. "So, start at the beginning, Sam. Tell us step by step how you ended up at the O'Connor farm and what happened there."

"Before we begin, I'd like to interject something," the lawyer said. She still held her pen in hand as though something important might happen and she'd need to jot it down. Her tweed suit and satin blouse were spotless and her severely short haircut offered a "give-me-no-nonsense" impression. "Since this case is new to me, and the charges so serious, I'll be reviewing the actions of your department very thoroughly. I suspect you've played fast and loose with the rule of law."

Kendra took in the woman's intent stare. Her rigid posture only added to her intensity. *Wow! I wouldn't want to be going up against her!*

The woman's statement seemed to have no effect on Deidre. "I'd be disappointed if you didn't, Jan. But you'll find we've crossed all our t's and dotted all our i's. Now, Sam, go ahead with your story. Don't have all day, y' know."

Edelson cleared his throat. "I'd heard talk around town that O'Connor had been saying racist things about Glory — even though she wasn't Latino. I guess just being married to Ricky was enough for the bigots in town. And from what I could tell, O'Connor was the leader of the whole damned bunch."

Deidre turned momentarily to Chucky. "You getting all this?"

He double-checked the camera. "Working good, chief."

She turned back to Edelson. "So, you never met the man? You were just acting on rumors?"

"Yeah, I wanted to find out if they were true. That's all. If they were, I was gonna ask for an apology."

Deidre frowned. "See, that's what I just don't get, Sam. Why'd you feel the need to defend her honor when she wasn't your wife?"

"Yeah, you're clueless. Haven't you ever loved anyone?" He gave her a contemptuous look. "This whole damned town and the way it operates has been gnawing at me for years. I was sick of the small mindedness and gossip. Then Glory moved to town and I could ignore all that crap. She was the only good thing in this miserable place. But then they started in about her — how she spent all her family's money on junk — how the house was filled with filth. It made my skin crawl whenever I heard another mean remark about her. She never did anything to hurt anyone — she was the closest thing to an angel you'd find on this planet." He hung his head.

His attorney placed a perfectly manicured hand on his back. "You all right, Sam?"

"Just give me a minute."

"So, what'd you do next?" Deidre asked after a heavy silence.

Edelson raised his head. "It was eating me alive —couldn't sleep — couldn't eat. I had to know if O'Connor was really saying those awful things about her. If he was, I had to fix it."

"So, on April 10ᵗʰ, you drove to his farm?"

"Yeah. When I got there, it was after supper time, but he was still working in the barn. He said, 'What you doin' here?' Hate oozed from the guy, even before he knew why I was there. I asked him if he knew who I was. Said he knew everyone in town and I was one of the shopkeepers, and what in the hell did I want. I said, 'I have a name. It's Sam Edelson.'"

Kendra heard a change in his voice. Something was building there.

"'So what?' the jerk asked me."

Edelson turned toward the mirror and she felt goosebumps on the back of her neck. *Does he know Mom and I are watching? No way. He doesn't even know the role we played in collecting his DNA. At least — not yet.* More tiny bumps popped up on her arms.

He returned his gaze to Deidre. "When I confronted him, he just laughed. Then he said, 'So, why're you worried about a dead Spic-lover? Far as I'm concerned, it's one less to worry about.' He gave me a dismissive wave and turned back to his work."

Sam picked up one of the water bottles and took a long drink. The transformation in his voice was complete now. It was low and ominous. "It was clear I'd never get an apology out of the old bastard. I grabbed him by the shoulders and spun him around. Hit him as hard as I could. He fell into a pile of hay." He cleared his throat. "I'd turned to go and was almost out of the barn when I looked back and saw him charging at me with a pitchfork." He looked at the chief, as if gauging her reaction.

Then he swiveled to his lawyer and a silent message seemed to pass between them. "Just before he reached me, his boot snagged on something and he fell onto the pitchfork. Swear to God, I didn't mean to hurt the guy, other than to give him a cut lip. He did it to himself."

Deidre said, "Hmm. Pretty good story. Too bad I don't believe it."

"Why not?" Jan asked. "Seems very plausible to me."

"Okay, so say it *was* an accident, why didn't you call for help?" the chief asked.

His voice morphed into a whine. "'Cuz I knew you wouldn't believe me. Besides, he wasn't hurt that bad. He was up on his knees and cussin' at me when I drove away."

"I might've believed you if you'd called then, but I sure don't now."

Ms. Emineth rose from her chair, snapped the latches on her briefcase, opened it with a curt flair, and tossed the papers and pen inside. "We're done here — not another word, Sam."

"Okay, but just to be clear, we're charging you with O'Connor's murder, as well as Glory's," Deidre said.

"You can't do that! I told you yesterday I'll sue you! And I will!"

Kendra stared at him in disbelief. *There's that rage again, lurking just beneath the surface of a calm exterior.*

"Won't be the first time," Deidre replied nonchalantly.

Jan grabbed her client's arm. "Be quiet, Sam." She turned to Chucky. "Turn off that camera, now!"

And just like that, the interview ended with Kendra and her mom shaking their heads in amazement.

Chapter 40

"**H**urry up," Audrey mouthed around her toothbrush. "I've got news."

The girls stood side by side in front of Audrey's bathroom mirror. Kendra couldn't help but notice the curves beneath her friend's pajama top. When she looked at her own reflection, she saw what resembled a young boy's shape. *I shouldn't be surprised. Audrey always outdoes me, from schoolwork to having everything a girl could want.* Then she scolded herself for being jealous. *Besides sharing her clothes and make up, she's stuck with me through most of my hare-brained ideas. Heck — she even broke into Grimsby's apartment with me. Dragging her feet all the way, of course, but she did it.*

She thought back to that day when her suspicion that Grimsby might be Cloud's killer changed to a certainty. She'd convinced Audrey they should follow him home on his lunch break to find out where he lived. When he left a short time later, she suggested they look around for a way to sneak into his apartment. At first, her friend was adamant they leave, but when she threatened to check it out by herself, her friend had caved. They found a door key behind a window flower box on the porch and crept through the apartment, looking for anything suspicious. They hit the jackpot in the bedroom where they found a gun, X-rated pictures, and worst of all — a cardboard box of girls' clothes, which appeared to be souvenirs from his murderous escapades. What she hadn't counted on was the monster's almost immediate return because he'd forgotten his lunch. Panic-stricken, they'd crouched in the bedroom closet while they listened to him slamming cupboard doors and muttering obscenities to himself. And when he'd left without a clue they were there, Audrey had totally lost it. Shoot, she'd been a mess herself. After they'd regained some of their composure, they'd run like the wind to get out of that place of horrors. *Yup, she's definitely the best friend I could ever wish for.*

Wiping the toothpaste from their chins, they hurried to Audrey's bedroom where they burrowed beneath the covers. Giggling, Kendra sat up, took her pillow and smacked her friend. "So, what's this big news?"

"Remember when I told you the Johnny and Shania thing wouldn't last?"

"Yeah." She held her breath.

"Well, they're history."

Something bubbled up inside. Something good. "Really? Who told you?"

"Lucas. He said Johnny got tired of conversations that only had to do with Shania fishing for compliments, or discussing how many calories are in a French fry."

She thought about the talks she and Johnny used to have. They certainly hadn't solved any of the world's craziness, but they'd shared better stuff than that. "Gosh."

"Is that all you can say? Come on, aren't you happy as snot?"

"Most definitely." A big smile bloomed on her face. Then the inevitable pillow fight began, and lasted until they fell into an exhausted heap. "I love sleepovers here."

"You're just sayin' that 'cuz I told you something you wanted to hear."

"You're right, but I always have a blast here. Wish I could do it more, but now that Mom's dating again, she expects me to watch Toni most weekends."

"I know, but why can't I spend the night at your place sometime? We could hang out while you're babysitting."

"You know I've only got a twin bed," Kendra said.

"Hey, I don't mind the floor. I could bring my sleeping bag."

She wondered why she hadn't thought of that. "I'll ask Mom if you can come over next weekend." They chattered on for a while about Johnny's breakup and the murder cases until Audrey got drowsy and rolled over on her side.

But, as usual, Kendra's eyes refused to close. The news about Johnny was big. *Will he want me back? And...do I want him back?* Now that some time had passed since Edelson had been arrested and his trial was set way in the future, he might forgive her for playing detective. She'd have to watch what she said in front of him, though. Deidre still kept her in the loop. "The district attorney will try to prove that O'Connor's death wasn't an accident," Deidre had informed her last week. "He'll claim that Edelson went to the O'Connor farm intending to kill the man who'd slandered the woman he loved."

"But, Ms. Emineth, attorney extraordinaire, will try to convince the jury that Glory's murder was a hate crime committed by O'Connor and his bigot friends. Then she'll probably come up with some story about O'Connor regretting what they'd done. And when he threatened to turn himself in, his so-called buddies killed him to shut him up."

"But Edelson confessed to killing Glory!"

"Welcome to the world of criminal law." Deidre had shrugged. "Defendants get an attorney and we start from square one. It's maddening. But we did everything by the book, and I think the confession's a lock."

Kendra had shook her head in disbelief.

"Anyway, back when we were looking at potential killers, Sam had pretty much thrown me off the trail with his 'upstanding-citizen act.' If you hadn't come up with your suspicions about the creep, he may've gotten away with it."

"Um, thanks. Question, though. What was the deal with the cologne?"

"Chucky and I noticed it at Glory's crime-scene and I knew it was something different. And lo and behold, when we searched his house, we found a bottle of the stuff on his dresser. It's purely circumstantial evidence and wouldn't hold up in court, but it was one more thing that convinced Chucky and me that we had the right guy. Anything else on your mind?"

"Yeah. Something's really bugging me — will Mom and I have to testify?"

"We'll do our best to keep you off the stand. But your mom will definitely have to tell how the DNA was collected."

As Kendra thought back to their conversation, she remembered how relieved she'd been to learn she was probably off the hook for appearing in court. The thought of having the killer stare darts at her as she testified gave her the heebie-jeebies. But she *was* hoping the case would be tried during summer break. It'd be so sweet to see a real trial, especially one where she'd helped bring in the killer.

Finally, she felt sleep overtaking her. Her mind drifted back to Johnny. As she slipped into nothingness, she remembered the sensation of his hand on the small of her back as they walked to class. *How sweet it would be to feel his touch again.*

Chapter 41

Kendra sat cross-legged on her narrow bed and scrolled through the clothes app on her iPhone. The town was planning a special potluck honoring her family for their part in bringing a murderer to justice. She could scarcely believe it, and the thought of it made her stomach churn. "Do I have to go? What if they expect me to get up and say something?" she'd grumbled to her mom. Just delivering an oral report in her English class made her jumpy.

"You're kidding, right?" Teresa had planted her hands on her hips. "The whole town's making a huge effort, and you're going to blow them off?" She shook her head. "Yet you have no trouble working side by side with someone you think might be a killer? Go figure!"

"Well, when you put it that way..." she'd said.

The potluck was only a week away and she wasn't just jittery about having to speak in public. What was she going to wear? She didn't have a thing. *I can always ask Audrey if I can borrow an outfit, but just once, I'd like something special of my own.* Now that she wasn't working at The Trading Post, all the money she earned from babysitting and mowing lawns went to pay her cell phone bill. She couldn't afford even the cheapest thing on the app. Tossing the phone on the bed, she went in search of a snack. Disappointment always made her hungry.

Returning to her room with a mouthful of peanut butter crackers, she found her sister on her bed, iPhone in hand. Choking the dryness of the crackers down, she mumbled, "What're you doing? You know you're not s'posed to touch my phone."

"Look what I did." Toni beamed and held it out to her. She grabbed the phone and stared wide-eyed at a very official-looking receipt on the screen. "Why'd you do that?" she yelled.

Toni's chin began to quiver. "You wanted a new dress — it's your favorite color — blue." Big tears formed on her long lashes.

She scrolled to the screen showing the dress. "OMG Toni! You ordered a 2X! And it's a soccer mom's dress!" She knew she was screaming, but couldn't stop. Through her anger, she heard laughter and turned to see her mom in the doorway. "What's so funny?"

"I don't know — maybe the thought of you in such a dress," Teresa replied. "Here, let me see it." She swiped back to the checkout screen. "Hmm, looks like the sale went through, but we should be able to return it. Not such a good idea to leave your phone lying around, huh?"

She bit her lip and shrugged. She knew her mom was right, but jeez — she was only gone a minute.

"So, you want something new for the potluck? My treat. In fact, I think we all deserve a new outfit. But we're going to a real store."

She shook her head to be sure she heard correctly. "Really?" she squeaked.

"Really," Teresa said.

Kendra's head hurt from the deafening noise. It seemed the whole town had turned out for the Award Potluck and everyone was talking at once. As she scanned the auditorium, she saw many of her classmates, some of her teachers, a few business people, and others known and unknown to her. And of course, Mrs. Snyderman, — the rude woman with the six brats who made her life miserable at The Trading Post,— was in attendance, and as usual, trying unsuccessfully to corral her unruly tribe.

She looked at the tables set up at the side of the room. They bent in the middle from the weight of all the food. There were salads of every description, slow cookers containing who knew what, pans of fried chicken, pork chops and roast beef, homemade pumpkin and zucchini breads, and yeasty rolls. The desserts claimed a long table all their own: every pie known to man, Meredith Smith's famous mile-high chocolate cake, all kinds of cookies, and raspberry cheesecake. Her stomach rumbled, but she wasn't sure if it was from hunger or nervousness. Deidre had assured her she wouldn't have to speak. "Just stand when you and your mother are acknowledged," she'd said. But she was still worried.

She glanced over at the table where her school friends were. She spied Johnny. It was the first time she'd been in the same room with him since Audrey had told her of the breakup. He must've felt her eyes on him, because he turned from his conversation with Lucas to look at her. Instead of casting his look aside, she continued to gaze at him. She felt powerless in his stare. A warmth bloomed inside of her. Suddenly, she realized she was grinning hugely. *Nothing like playing the fool.*

The sound of the mayor's voice calling for quiet saved her, and she turned and headed to the table where the town officials, Ricky and Alex Delgado, and her family were sitting. She couldn't help but notice that Alex actually looked happy. *Maybe he's starting to put all the bad stuff behind him.*

"All right," the mayor said, rubbing his hands together in front of his more-than-ample belly, "we're going to keep this short and sweet, because as you can see, we've got some mighty good-looking dishes. And I, for one, can't wait to dig into them. So, here's Chief Goodwin to do the honors." His folding chair creaked dangerously beneath his weight as he settled back in his seat.

Deidre rose from her place between the mayor and Kendra's mom. "You all know we're here tonight to honor the Morgan family for their part in helping to keep Finchville safe. In an effort to help us apprehend Glory Delgado and Robert O'Connor's killer, they went well beyond what could be expected of anyone. And I'm sure you're aware that Kendra was instrumental in solving Cloud Nicholson's murder last year. We owe them more than we can possibly repay. As a small token of our gratitude, we're making them both honorary deputies." The chief picked up two badges from the table. "Please stand up, you two."

The room burst into thunderous applause as Deidre pinned the badges on them. Kendra was sure her cheeks were the color of Mom's new red dress.

"And even though Kendra was accepted as a cadet in the department months ago, since she was working undercover, she couldn't wear a cadet uniform. So, it's a little late, but here it is." Deidre handed her a cellophane-wrapped package.

She tried to make out the details of the uniform, but her eyes were blurry.

Then the chief did something very surprising — she hugged each of them. "Oh, and one more thing. I almost forgot another very important person in the Morgan household. Toni, would you stand please?"

Toni leapt from her seat. She was so short, her head barely showed above the table.

Deidre took her by the hand and led her around to where all could see. She retrieved a small plastic version of Teresa and Kendra's badges from her pocket and pinned it to her ruffled dress. "Toni, you are now a Finchville deputy, too." She then gave the delighted little girl a kiss on the cheek. Again, the room erupted in applause.

"All right, that's it for the speech making. Please wait for our town's important guests and officials to get their food, and then proceed according to your table number, starting with Table 1. Thanks so much for showing your support for our town heroes by providing us with your marvelous food and valued presence."

Teresa beamed at Kendra as they headed over to get their food. Suddenly, she was ravenous. She piled her plate as full as possible before stopping by the table with sodas and water. "Shall I get Toni a bottle of water?" she called to her mom.

"Sure."

That wasn't half-bad. Don't know what I was worried about. Kendra forked potato salad into her mouth. *I wonder what I'd have to do to rate another one of these parties?* she joked to herself. Throughout the dinner, people came up to congratulate her and her family. Her sister was so excited she barely ate a mouthful. Although she had trouble graciously accepting the many compliments, Toni didn't.

She'd look at them and answer in earnest. "Yes, it was very scary!" or, "We knew it was the right thing to do.", as if she'd actually been there.

She tried not to burst out laughing. *What an imagination.* Of course, Toni had been unaware of what was happening with the cases while they were unfolding, but she'd certainly been tuned into the discussions afterward, and was more than willing to take credit now. *The kid will probably have a career in politics someday.*

Finally, the party wound down and people began retrieving their empty serving dishes. Her mom had gone to the kitchen for plastic wrap so she could take Toni's plate home. She hadn't talked to Johnny yet, but now she saw him heading her way. She told her lungs to draw a breath. They refused.

"Wanna go outside a minute?"

Finally, she sucked in some air. "Um, sure. Soon as my mom gets back."

Before Teresa could get all the way back to the table, Toni was yelling. "Mama, Ken'ra's boyfrien' wants to talk to her! Outside!"

She resisted the urge to strangle her sister.

"Toni, use your indoor voice," Teresa said, and then to Kendra, "You go on, honey. We'll wait for you."

She draped her sweater over her shoulders and stepped into the night air. It was blissfully cool on her hot cheeks. Johnny took her elbow and steered her away from the crowd. His touch made her feel woozy. "So, how've you been?" *Could I sound anymore stupid?*

"Good," he said. "Well, maybe not so good."

"Oh?"

He cleared his throat and bounced up and down on his toes. "Think I made a mistake, letting you go."

"Hmm."

"Yeah. Didn't like your detectiving, or whatever you call it."

"I remember." She felt her usual confidence returning when she realized he was as nervous as she was.

"But that's over now. Right? Look, I miss talkin' to you and the other stuff."

She thought about making him even more uncomfortable by asking what he meant by "the other stuff," but decided that'd be mean. Instead, she wanted to launch herself into his arms, but something held her back. *It was true the case was closed, but what if another one came up?* Then she realized what a silly idea that was. It'd been mind-boggling that Finchville had had two killers in a short time, when in its entire history, no other murders were on record. "I miss you, too," she admitted.

He sighed and gathered her to him.

Then she realized something else was nagging at her. "But are you sure you don't mind that I don't fit into the cool club, like Shania, and her posse?"

"Oh, Kenny, you gotta be kidding. Haven't missed her and her snooty friends, even a second. I'd be real bothered if you were anything like them."

She couldn't have hoped for a more perfect ending to an already perfect day.

Chapter 42

Months had passed. Spring was here and Grimsby's trial hadn't even started yet, let alone Edelson's. *Geez, by the time their trials are underway, I'll be in the market for wrinkle creams.* She was so deep in thought about her last conversation with Deidre that the sweet smell of lilacs crowding the sidewalk was lost on Kendra.

The chief had repeated that her testimony wouldn't be needed in the Delgado/O'Connor trial. "I'm sure the jury won't fall for that story about O'Connor falling on his pitchfork — it's so ludicrous. Edelson's intent is really the only issue for the jury to decide, and in his taped conversation, he was clear that he was avenging Glory's honor. First, he kills her, then he defends her. What a mental case! His attorney is excellent, but there are just some things which can't be overcome."

"Grimsby is the one I've got concerns about." Deidre's brow had furrowed. "Besides abducting you, and killing Cloud, we suspect him of other murders. This guy is really dangerous and I want him put away forever. And unlike Edelson, he won't talk — he's a slippery S.O.B. Would you be willing to get on the stand against him, if necessary?"

She thought about Grimsby and how terrified she'd been when he kidnapped her. She gulped. "Don't know." She looked around the room, knowing there was no escape from what Deidre was asking. "I guess I could do it if it's the only way to be sure he never hurts anyone again." Just being an onlooker in both courtrooms was all she really wanted. Watching Edelson's interrogations last fall had been fascinating and she was sure the trials would be, too. But her fear of testifying against Grimsby made her ribs hurt and her lungs contract.

"Don't sound very sure of yourself. Well, we'll cross that bridge when we come to it. Maybe we'll have more than enough to give him several life sentences." Deidre had given her a reassuring pat on the back.

As she continued on toward home, she thought about her upcoming sixteenth birthday. Her mom had been bugging her to take driver's ed. classes, but she really didn't understand why. They didn't have a car. And just paying her cell phone bill kept her broke most of the time. Even if Mom came up with the money for a used car, there'd be no way for her to pay her own insurance, let alone buy gas.

Her mom was collecting Toni from daycare so that meant she was down for dinner prep. Turning her key in the lock, she entered the empty apartment, threw her backpack on the bed, and put on her new favorite pop artist. She hummed along as she chopped tomatoes and lettuce for tacos. Then she grated cheese and laid out the taco shells. Over the sizzle of the frying hamburger she heard them burst through the door, Toni chattering like the little magpie she was. Mom rolled her eyes at Kendra and they laughed together.

"What?" Toni stopped talking and looked back and forth at them.

"Nothing, sweetie. Go wash up and you can help set the table," Teresa said.

The tacos were delicious. She was piling the sour cream on her third one when Mom said, "My sister's calling from Phoenix tonight. You going to be around?"

"Just doing homework. Want me to entertain Toni so you can talk?"

"Sure."

She'd barely spread her books out on the table before the land line rang and Teresa picked up. She watched her mom carry the handset into the tiny living room. She thought it was strange her aunt was calling again so soon. They'd just talked last week. By Mom's own admission, they'd never been close. A few minutes passed and Teresa walked back into the kitchen and extended the phone. "Your aunt wants to talk to you."

"Me?" She felt her eyes widen.

"Yup."

"Hi-i-i Aunt Lena. How are you?"

"I'm good, Kendra. Busy as ever. Wish people would stop thinking of ways to kill each other. But then I guess I'd be out of a job." She laughed.

She giggled at her aunt's dark humor.

"Your mom's been telling me all about your sleuthing activities. A little young for that, aren't you?"

Oh no, she's going to get on my case. "Guess so, but I can't seem to stay away from it."

"That's what I hear. I was concerned when your mom first told me about it. That was, until I talked to the head of the police department there. She gave me a lot of detail about what you've been up to. Says they probably couldn't have closed their cases without you. And she said you're even learning not to take such crazy chances — although you still need to work on that."

"She did?" Her nervousness morphed to pleasure.

"Yeah. Sounds like you've got a knack for police work. But it *is* a very dangerous profession and I don't want my niece getting hurt — or worse. So, I was thinking it'd be a good idea for you to spend the summer with me."

"Really?" She thought she must be hearing things.

"Yeah, you could learn a lot by shadowing me. But I'll warn you now — I'm a taskmaster and you won't be going off on your own and doing anything stupid."

She could tell by her aunt's tone of voice that she meant what she said. She managed to stammer, "I'll follow all the rules, for sure."

"Okay, I'll take care of your round-trip flight, and maybe I can even talk my boss into giving you a small stipend. But don't count on it. The man thinks he invented money and there's only a limited supply."

She heard her Aunt Lena take a breath. "All right. Hand the phone back to your mom so we can get started on the arrangements."

Her mind buzzed with her dumb luck. She was staring stupidly at a blank wall when her mom signed off and joined her at the table.

"You look shocked, Kendra. Guess I should've given you a hint of what was coming. But I wanted you to be surprised."

"Well, you nailed it, Mom."

"That's why I wanted you to start on your driver's training," Teresa continued. "Lena has two cars and if you have your license, she might need you to drive sometimes."

"Drive — in Phoenix?" She was moving from shocked to stunned. "Isn't that a huge city? The traffic would be horrendous."

"True, but she lives in one of the suburbs. It's less busy there. She'd probably just want you to run to the store and stuff."

"Wow! I can't believe this is really happening!" She jumped up, ran around the table and gave her mom a giant hug.

Chapter 43

Kendra's heartbeat catapulted against her chest as fast as Johnny's dad's ancient pickup truck's rattle. They were headed to the Grand Island Airport and she hadn't counted on being this undone about going to the big city. She hoped her nerves would settle once they left the gravel road and hit the highway. Since her aunt's call, the time had both flown and dragged by. Now the day was actually here.

One thing that had helped the time go faster were her driving classes. When she was ready to take the actual test, Peg Strong had been kind enough *and brave enough* to make her Nissan available. She'd worried about remembering to stay under the speed limit and to signal when she changed lanes. And she'd been doubly freaked at the prospect of being tested in someone else's car, but Peg had reassured her that she'd placed a call to her insurance company for temporary coverage for a guest driver. In spite of the fact that she'd knocked over an orange traffic cone while trying to parallel park, she'd passed the test and was now the proud owner of a Nebraska state driver's license. And now she was heading for Phoenix!

She glanced over at Johnny and saw his clenched jaw. He wasn't only bummed that she was leaving for the summer, but that her aunt was actually encouraging her to pursue a career in law enforcement. They'd argued about it many times, but nothing was holding her back. She knew he was hurt and plenty angry. But he'd still jumped at the chance to drive her to the airport.

She'd said her goodbyes to her mom and sister that morning. She knew the sacrifice Mom was making by letting her go — daycare was pricey, and now Toni would be there a lot more. Plus, there'd be no one to help with the chores. She'd gotten teary as she tried to say thank you. Teresa had interpreted her tears as fear of the trip — and it was true she was terrified about flying for the first time, and if she'd get along with her aunt — but she also knew she'd miss her family like crazy.

"You know, if you don't like it there, you don't have to stay the whole summer." Teresa hugged her.

"I think I'll be okay, Mom. Feel bad about leaving you with all the work though."

Teresa laughed. "Hey, that's the joy of being a grownup, right?"

"Ken'ra, I wanna go with you. I'm a depity!" Toni pointed to the toy badge pinned to her shirt.

She's gonna wear that thing out. She never takes it off. "I know you are. But Aunt Lena just invited me this time. Maybe you can go next time."

Toni stuck out her lower lip and crossed her arms over her chest. "But I wanna go *now!*"

"Tell you what. I'll bring you something super-cool back. What would you like from Arizona?"

Toni perked up. Then she lowered her head and put her hand on her forehead like she was thinking.

She smiled at Toni's typical theatrics.

"I know. A puppy. Brown — he has to be brown."

Teresa stepped behind Toni and frantically shook her head back and forth.

Noting Mom's panic, she said, "A puppy might be kinda hard to get on the plane. I promise I'll find something you'll love though, okay?" She pulled her onto her lap and kissed her cheek. "And of course, I'll call you all the time. Come on, you can help me finish packing."

"Well, here we are." Johnny interrupted her thoughts. As he pulled into a parking space, he added, "We're early — let's sit in the truck for a while."

She felt her stomach clench as she saw a huge jet sitting on the runway. The thought of actually getting on that death trap slammed into her like a boulder. And the airport terminal was tiny — *do they really know what they're doing?* "O-o-okay," she stammered.

He turned to her. "You're not scared, are you? Not the oh-so-fearless police cadet?"

"Don't start up again. Please, Johnny."

"Your teeth are almost chattering. In June, yet." He pulled her to him and stroked her hair. "It'll be okay, baby." He lifted her chin and kissed her gently on the lips.

She felt her fear subside a notch. "I'll miss you so much. I promise — I'll call or text every day."

"You'd better." His tone was light, but she knew he meant it.

They cuddled a while longer until it was time to check in. Johnny swung her two bags from the back of the truck and they entered the terminal. The check-in line was directly in front of them. She felt her stomach spasms return.

The queue moved at lightning speed and suddenly they were at the ticket counter with a harried-looking woman demanding her boarding pass and identification. She curtly motioned Johnny to place one bag at a time on a large metal scale where another worker looped adhesive strips on each handle, pulled them from the scale, and tossed them onto a moving conveyer belt. After briefly inspecting her driver's license, the woman handed it back to her along with her boarding pass. She pointed in the direction of the security checkpoint.

An imposing uniformed man stood behind a podium. He reached for her paperwork and inspected her and the picture on her license. Satisfied, he handed the items back to her and put his hand up to stop Johnny. "You can't go past this point."

She swallowed and turned to face him. With the TSA guard watching, he bent and gave her a huge kiss. When they broke apart, she saw the man was smiling.

She kept peering over her shoulder to see Johnny as she moved along the line. Others were taking off their shoes, so she did, too. She placed her phone and purse with them in a plastic tub. It was getting harder and harder to see Johnny as she went forward. If only she were taller. Finally, she jumped up and down for one last glimpse, spotted him, and waved as she was jostled forward in the crowd.

Thirty minutes later, after waiting in a packed room with crying babies and people feverishly talking on cell phones, she found herself aboard the plane in her window seat. She was amazed to look out and see Johnny standing at the chain-link fence. She waved again. He saw her and waved back. Her chest hurt, like when she swallowed a gulp of soda too fast. *I hate leaving him. This must be what love feels like. But if it's really love, would I be able to go to Phoenix for the summer? Oh, who am I kidding? I know it'd be impossible to be a farmer's wife, raising crops and babies. I'd go stark raving bonkers. No, I want the big city — where big things happen — where I can help somebody — bring some sort of peace to people like Alex and Ricky Delgado. Why can't Johnny understand that?*

As the plane started to taxi and Johnny faded from view, she pushed her troubled thoughts aside and turned her attention to the prospect ahead of her — surviving this flight. *If this big metal box goes down in a spectacular fireball, my measly problems won't matter.* Acid climbed its way from the pit of her stomach and she began frantically looking for the barf bag Mom had told her would be in the seat pocket.

Acknowledgements

Again, I find myself indebted to family and friends for their support, especially to those who kept asking, "When is your next book coming out?" They kept me motivated when the going got rocky.

To my faithful editor, Teresa Becker: your assistance in copy and content editing was unsurpassed.

A grateful shout out goes to Reed Anderson, Retired Deputy, for the King County, Washington Sheriff Reserve, and Timothy Moore, Retired Detective, for the Phoenix, Arizona Police Department. Your knowledge of law enforcement provided me with the information I needed about DNA, Miranda warnings, and much more.

A big thank you to Bill Konigsberg, Writer-in-Residence for the Mesa Public Library, who helped me provide the reader with a clear picture of story setting.

And to Jan Emineth, who allowed me to use her name for the character of the defense attorney, I hope you enjoy her portrayal.

Finally, a huge thank you to Robin Cain and Thomas Spille for once again slogging through the first draft of the story and not telling me to get a nine to five job.

Made in the USA
San Bernardino, CA
20 August 2017